BEWARE!!
DO NOT READ THIS
BOOK FROM
BEGINNING TO END!

When a genie named Jenna pops out of a soda can and offers you three wishes, you think all your dreams have come true. But Jenna has a few tricks up her sleeve. If you don't watch out, the wishes of your dreams could turn into a nightmare!

Should you wish to to be rich? Famous? The best-looking kid around? Or—something else entirely? It's up to you. But when you decide—be careful. Jenna's wishes have a way of going wrong. You could find yourself battling an evil ninja rat-man. Or trapped on a desert island. Or chased by a tiger!

Oh, and one more thing. If you don't say your wish exactly the right way . . . Jenna will see you to your doom!

You're in control of this scary adventure. You decide what will happen. And how terrifying the scares will be!

Start on PAGE 1. Then follow the instructions at the bottom of each page. You make the choices.
SO TAKE A DEEP BREATH, CROSS YOUR FINGERS, AND TURN TO PAGE 1 TO *GIVE YOURSELF GOOSEBUMPS!*

READER BEWARE —
YOU CHOOSE THE SCARE!

Look for more
GIVE YOURSELF GOOSEBUMPS adventures
from R.L. STINE

R.L. STINE
GIVE YOURSELF

SCREAM OF THE EVIL GENIE

AN
APPLE
PAPERBACK

SCHOLASTIC INC.
New York Toronto London Auckland Sydney

A PARACHUTE PRESS BOOK

ISBN 0-590-84773-2

12 11 10 9 8 7 6 5 4 3 2 1   7 8 9/9 0 1 2/0

Printed in the U.S.A.   40

First Scholastic printing, January 1997

"Anybody home?" you call, charging into your house after school one day. The door bangs shut behind you.

Silence. Total silence.

"Hello? Mom? Dad? Anybody?"

No answer.

Weird, you think. You drop your schoolbooks on the living-room table and hurry toward the kitchen.

Why is there no one around? Not even your brother or sister. You've never come home and found the place empty.

Your footsteps creak on the floor as you head for the kitchen door.

"Mom?" you call again. Nothing.

You feel a little creepy all alone in the house. Then you think of something that makes you grin.

No one's here — you can do anything you want!

Time to raid the refrigerator!

You zoom into the kitchen and yank open the fridge door.

Yes! It's packed. There's some leftover pizza, a whole container of nacho cheese sauce, chocolate cake, a big bottle of fruit punch, two six-packs of cola, and fried chicken legs.

You're reaching for some cake when something catches your eye.

Hey — did one of those cola cans move?

Go on to PAGE 2.

You stare at the cola can. Nothing happens.

It's only a can of soda, you tell yourself. The silence must be getting to you.

You grab the cola from the six-pack, along with some chips and a slab of chocolate cake. Why not? You don't usually have a chance to pig out like this!

Then you head for the family room. You flop down on the couch in front of the TV. No battle over the remote today!

Where is everybody, anyway? you wonder again.

You flip up the tab on the cola can to open it. Instantly you hear the fizzy gas escaping.

PSSSSSSSSSSSSSSSS.

Whoa! The fizzing won't stop! You shove the can away from you, holding it out away from your body. The can must have been shaken up.

A fine wet spray shoots out all over you. Then a cloud of misty white gas begins escaping from the can. Your eyes widen as the cloud grows bigger and bigger. It fills the room like a giant mushroom cloud.

Your mouth drops open in awe.

Something *else* is coming out of the can!

Something alive!

Go on to PAGE 3.

With a loud hissing sound, a ghostly, life-sized young woman squeezes out of the cola can and floats in front of you.

"Ouch!" she exclaims. She shakes herself off like a wet dog. The mist scatters around her. "That hurt!"

For another second, she hovers above the coffee table. Her form is thin and airy, like a hologram.

Then she suddenly becomes solid. She drops to the ground and lands on her two feet with a thud.

"Hi!" she greets you. "What's up?"

You don't answer her. You can't. You're too shocked to make your mouth move.

Instead, you stare at the amazing person standing in your family room. She's got spiky red-and-purple hair and five earrings. She's wearing a fuzzy, short black sweater and baggy blue jeans with black combat boots.

"Hey! I'm talking to you!" she yells.

Go on to PAGE 4.

4

"Uh, hi," you answer. You're too surprised to say much else.

She's cool, you think, watching her strut around as if she owns the place. Definitely cool.

"Nice place — sort of!" she exclaims with a snorty kind of laugh. She flops down in a big stuffed chair across from you, stretches her legs out, and lets her combat boots fall on the coffee table with a clunk. She flashes you a big smile.

"Okay, let's cut to the chase," she rattles off. "My name's Jenna. I'm a genie — and you've got three wishes. Boom. Boom. Boom. Whatever you want. Three things. Fame, fortune, a giant bag of diamond rings — you name it. Except I don't do windows. And I don't do guns, knives, or death. If you want to off someone, get another genie. Got that?"

"Uh, yeah," you mutter, finding your voice.

"So what's it going to be? Make your first wish," she insists.

Go on to PAGE 5.

Before you can ask one of the zillion questions swimming around in your brain, Jenna snaps her fingers.

"Oops! Wait," she cries. "There's something I forgot to tell you. The most important part. When you want to make another wish, you've got to open the cola can again. Then *WHOOSH!* I'll pop out and say 'What's up?' and we can boogie from there. Got it?"

"No!" You shake your head hard. "I don't get *any* of this. How did you get into that can in the first place? And how can I open it again if it's already open? And how can you come out again? You're *already* out."

"It's a genie thing," Jenna explains with a toss of her head. "Believe me — I'll be in there. Take my word for it."

You're too astonished to argue with her. Is this for real?

"Okay, hurry up," Jenna says. "Make a wish. I don't have all day."

If you wish to be a big celebrity, turn to PAGE 73.

If you wish to be the richest kid in the world, turn to PAGE 45.

If you wish to be the best-looking kid in the world, turn to PAGE 39.

If you wish for something else besides money, fame, or good looks, turn to PAGE 66.

Ride the tiger? Not a chance, you decide.

That parrot must be out of his tiny, green-feathered skull!

Instead, you decide to follow Jenna on foot. You think it's much safer that way.

In a flash, you race off into the jungle, following the trail of smashed trees and torn branches that Jenna is leaving behind with every step she takes.

She's not too far ahead of you . . .

Which is a shame.

Because a moment later, she decides to turn around and see whether you're catching up to her.

She stops in her tracks, pivots, and . . .

"OWWWWW!"

That was you, speaking — or rather screaming — your last word.

Remember how you thought she could squash you like a bug, just by moving one foot?

Well, she just did.

THE END

You're still shaking with fear. But you decide you've got to face whatever's in that jungle if you're going to have any hope of finding the cola can.

Slowly you walk toward the trees. The hair on the back of your neck stands up.

Dark, dense vines hang down, casting strange shadows. You push the vines back, and enter the jungle of palm trees, bushes, and tropical flowers.

The scent of the jungle is sweet. A warm flowery smell fills the air. Small prickly bushes scratch your legs. Sunlight streams through the trees every so often, in bold beams.

You glance down, searching the ground for the cola can.

"AWWWWK!"

You jump when you hear the sharp cry. It's followed by a rapid flapping sound.

Your head snaps up. Out of the corner of your eye, you see something moving. A screeching winged creature — heading right for your face!

Duck out of the way on PAGE 28!

You decide to let James do all the work. He can open the cola cans for you. Why not? What else are servants for?

"Uh, James." You're not sure how to explain. "This is going to sound crazy, but ... "

You take a deep breath and tell him all about the genie. About how she made you rich, but now she's locked inside a cola can and you don't know which one.

"So could you open all the cola cans for me, James, until you find her? Just pour out the ones that are really cola — we can always buy more. When you find her, let me know," you instruct him.

"Of course," James replies, although he looks at you as if you're crazy. "But don't try sneaking away again. I'm keeping an eye on you, remember?"

James disappears into the pantry, and you settle down in the family room with your favorite afternoon TV show. The screen is so big, it's like watching a movie!

Two hours later you wonder — what's taking James so long?

Did something go wrong?

Go on to PAGE 29.

"Get back!" you yell. "Get away, you slimy creep!"

The rat-man's swords whirl so fast they're just a silver blur. Desperate, you pick up another brick and hurl it. It hits him smack in the gut. Hard.

"ARWOWGHH!" the rat-man cries. He drops his swords and doubles over in pain, clutching his stomach. His shoulders heave as if he's about to be sick. He opens his mouth . . .

. . . and belches.

Gross! you think. Then you notice that something shiny has popped out of his mouth. A cola can!

Could it be *your* cola can? With the genie inside?

You lunge forward, grab the can, and rip off the top. White smoke pours out, then forms itself into Jenna's shape.

"I wish—" you start to say.

But that's as far as you get.

"HIYAAAHHH!" the rat-man screeches. You look up—and see his swords slicing through the air. Right at your head.

Hey! How'd he pick them up so fast?

You didn't really think you could beat a ninja rat-man, did you? The most horrifying warrior in all of Mortal Revenge?

Oh, well. Better luck next game!

THE END

You stare into the snake's tiny eyes. You hear the genie laugh and snap his fingers.

POOF. POOF. POOF.

Instantly, you are surrounded by three more giant poisonous rattlesnakes, almost as big as the first. They all bare their fangs, dripping venom.

The poison pools on the tile floor in the pantry. It starts seeping toward your feet. You can't believe what's happening.

You scrunch up your toes. You pull your shoulders in, trying to make yourself smaller. But the snakes close in.

HISSSSS! The largest one opens its jaws even wider. In two seconds, your head will be inside its mouth.

"Help me!" you squeak in a tiny voice.

"Sure. Just make a wish," the genie says with a cruel laugh.

Fear fills every blood vessel in your body. You can't think clearly. All you want is to get away — far away!

"I wish . . . I wish . . . I wish I were any place but here!" you cry, still frozen to your spot.

POOF!

Turn to PAGE 12.

You rush to the window to see what's going on outside.

Yeow!

You fly backward as a pane of glass explodes. A long metallic leg — with a metal pincer-claw — shoots into the house through the broken window.

You scream.

Randy screams.

Katie screams. "Make it go away!"

From the front yard, you hear Randy's friends shouting and yelling too.

The horrible metallic insect lifts itself up over the window sill. It lets out a shrill cry. Then it lands on your family-room floor.

Your eyes grow huge and your heart pounds horribly. Randy has backed up against a wall. Katie collapses to the ground.

"Why didn't it go away!" Katie wails. "I wished it would go away!"

You realize what happened. Katie didn't wish carefully enough. It went away, all right. Away to your front lawn.

And now it's back.

Turn to PAGE 60.

WHOOSH!

A burst of smoke blinds you. You feel yourself hurtling through space.

"Wait!" you cry out.

But it's too late.

When the spinning and tumbling finally stop, a cool refreshing breeze blows on your face. Your eyes pop open, and you shake your head to clear it.

"Wow!" you cry out, excited. "The beach!"

You hear a soft lapping sound — the sound of water gently licking the shore. Cool island breezes blow through your hair. A salty smell fills your nose.

You shield your eyes from the sun, squinting to take in the fabulous scene before you.

Sand. Palm trees. Rocks. Aqua-blue water so clear, you can see the brightly-colored fish darting just beneath the surface.

This is great! you think. I love the beach!

Then you glance behind you. Beside you. All around.

There's nobody there. No one. No genie. No nothing.

The place seems deserted.

You are totally alone!

Go on to PAGE 23.

A cold, scary feeling in your stomach tells you that you'd better find that cola can before you do anything else.

So you ignore your little sister's cries. She screams all the time anyway.

You approach the guy in the orange T-shirt.

"Uh, hey, that's my cola," you tell him. "I mean, I *think* it is. Where did you get it?"

"Whoa!" The guy holds up his hands and takes a step back. "Talk about paranoid! It's just a soft drink, kid. There are plenty of them in the kitchen. Check out the fridge."

"I know," you say. "I know. But, uh, I need a certain one. The one that was on the coffee table."

"No big deal." The guy shrugs. "You want it? You got it."

He tosses you the can. Is it the one?

You turn away from the guy and pop open the top.

No whoosh. No fizzing sound. Nothing pops out.

You sigh. It must just be a can of cola. So you start to take a sip.

Then you freeze, the can lifted to your lips. Your heart stops.

You don't believe it.

From inside the can, you hear a tiny, blood-curdling scream.

Turn to PAGE 86.

FFFZZZSSSSSST!

The can in your hand shoots away from you like a rocket. A white cloud of gas escapes, and then the genie.

"Whoa!" you exclaim. "What happened to you?"

Everything about Jenna is different this time. She's much bigger and she's wearing black leather instead of a fuzzy, soft black sweater. Her jacket has sharp metal studs sticking out all over. Even her boots look dangerous. There are some kind of sharp metal points on the toes.

Jenna looks as if she could hurt you just by giving you a hug.

"So," she says with a sneer. "Guess you aren't so good at this wishing thing, are you?"

"Uh, I never said anything about curling," you reply, trying to stand up for yourself. "I just wanted to be a sports star."

"And I made you a sports star," Jenna responds.

"But I — "

"*GRRRRRR,*" Jenna growls and you stop protesting.

When she bares her teeth, you see that they're sharply pointed. She holds her face up close to yours and growls again.

Turn to PAGE 33.

"Help!" you scream. You fling your arms over your head and squeeze your eyes shut tight. Your heart hammers so hard, you think your chest will burst.

Then you hear a loud thud. Behind you.

"Open your eyes," the parrot squawks. "Get the cola can."

Huh?

Slowly, you open your eyes and realize that the tiger leaped *over* you — not *at* you! You hear him panting right behind you. You can feel his hot breath on your neck.

"Get the cola can," the parrot repeats.

With your heart still pounding, you try to do what the parrot says. You slowly approach the cola machine. You push the quarters into the slot and hit the button.

KA-CHUNK. A can thumps down the chute and rolls out into your waiting hand. Nervously, you flip open the metal tab.

Pfft.

"Oh no!" you wail. "No genie! It's just cola!"

Now you'll never get off the island!

Turn to PAGE 26.

16

A bunch of Randy's friends stand in your front yard.

"How did that happen?" you hear them asking each other. "Did you see the sky go dark? Where did that metal thing go?"

Too hard to explain, you think.

But the important thing is, the monster is nowhere to be seen.

You turn back to the living room and stare at the mess.

Broken glass. Pizza boxes. Cola cans everywhere.

Empty cola cans. Not full ones.

"Close one," Randy declares, scrambling to his feet. "You used your last wish. Thanks."

"Yeah," you say a little sadly. Then you spot Jenna. She's sitting cross-legged on top of your family's big TV. She looks sad too.

"Oh, well." She sighs. "If I have to get stuck with a real job — being a *real* mom forever — I guess this isn't so bad. I'd rather have you guys than any of the other kids I've met."

"But you *are* our real mom," Randy says.

Not really, you think. Your real mom is in a cola can somewhere. And Jenna will never be able to get her back. Her genie powers have come to an

END.

You head for the food court. You can't resist buying a few things along the way: a ring for your mother, a CD Walkman for your brother, a stuffed dinosaur for your sister, and a shower radio for your dad. At each store you tell the clerk to "keep the change." It's fun to see their shocked faces when you do!

At the food court, you pile your tray high with all your favorite junk food. Peter does the same thing.

The cashier tells you you're going to get sick eating all that. But you just smile back and hand her a hundred-dollar-bill. "Keep the change," you tell her. Then you follow Peter to a table.

"Shopping is a great way to work up an appetite," you joke.

"I know what you mean." Peter takes a slurp of his chocolate shake. He glances past you. "That's weird," he mutters.

"What?" You turn around in your chair to see what he's staring at. A small crowd is gathering at the edge of the food court. Some of them point at you.

"Aren't those the salespeople from the stores we were in?"

You gaze at the group. "I think you're right," you murmur. "I wonder what they want?"

You won't have to wonder long if you turn to PAGE 126.

You decide to go on living with a blue face. Why not?

You don't want to waste one of your three wishes just to turn your face back to its regular color. And besides — your new mom has red-and-purple hair. A blue face will fit right in!

There's only one thing that's bothering you. . . .

"Uh, M-m-mom?" you stammer. It's weird calling Jenna by that name. "Uh, how come my face turned blue when Randy made a wish?"

"I'm giving him two wishes," she answers you. "Or maybe three. Or four! I'm not sure. Maybe I'll like him better than you."

"You can't do that!" you cry.

"Who says?" Jenna replies.

Randy's mouth is open so wide, it's hanging down to his chest. Finally he closes it enough to talk.

"Give me a break," Randy says, looking at you. "You don't really believe Mom can grant wishes. You don't think *I* did that, do you? Like, if I say, I wish that your face will be pink-and-yellow stripes, it's going to turn — WHOA!"

Turn to PAGE 106.

"Okay," you tell the young woman with the clipboard. "I'll get into my costume. Just give me a minute."

"Don't you want some help?" she asks, sounding surprised.

You shake your head. "No. I can do it myself."

Boy, were you wrong!

For the next twenty minutes, you struggle to get into the pink-and-green dragon suit. It's a joke. A really *bad* joke. The body part of the costume is stiff, hot, and hard to zip up. And the head? It's so heavy, it's like wearing a blanket!

Finally, you stumble out onto the soundstage to face a mob of antsy, squirming preschoolers. They clap and chant as soon as they spot you.

"Wilfred! Wilfred! Wilfred!" You never knew four-year-olds could be so loud!

The TV lights are even hotter than the lights in your dressing room. Sweat trickles into your eyes. You try to blink away the sting, but it doesn't help.

The headpiece isn't only hot and heavy — it's also much too big for you. It keeps slipping and sliding around, banging into your nose. Sometimes the eyeholes don't line up with your eyes.

You can't stand it! You rip the costume head off.

Uh-oh. Big mistake.

Turn to PAGE 113.

"Shut up!" Jenna bellows. "Nothing's happened to me! This is what I really look like. Got a problem with that?"

"No!" you respond hastily. "Of course not!"

Jenna narrows her cat-eyes at you and bares her fangs.

"What . . . do . . . you . . . WANT?" she demands, spitting each word out slowly.

What *do* I want? you wonder. With this new, scary Jenna in front of you, and a panting tiger behind you, you can't think straight!

But you've noticed one thing for sure. Every time you make a wish, it turns out wrong. Not at all how you expected. You know you're going to have to word your last wish very carefully.

Finally, you figure out what you're going to say.

"Here's what I want," you say to Jenna. "I want to go home, and have everything be just the way it was before you came along. Except for one thing. I want to remember all the amazingly cool stuff that's happened to me. Okay?"

"Are you *sure* that's what you want?" Jenna sneers. "Maybe you'd better wish that tiger would go away. He's about ready to attack!"

Quick, if you save yourself from the tiger, turn to PAGE 36.

If you bravely refuse to change your wish, turn to PAGE 62.

"Are you sure that's the right wish?" you demand.

Jenna just shrugs.

Smash!

The back door splinters into pieces. The monster!

"Okay," you cry. "I wish I never met you, Jenna."

For an instant, the world is dark. Spinning. Finally everything is still. You open your eyes — and find your mother standing beside you. Your regular mom!

Except you notice she's wearing funny clothes. You glance down. So are you.

You gaze at your mother again. You realize her clothing resembles the costumes worn in the Thanksgiving pageant at your school. She looks just like a Pilgrim.

Uh-oh.

"Um, excuse me?" you begin uncertainly. "What's your name?"

She laughs. "You know my name, silly. It's Lavinia."

Lavinia? That's the name of your great-great-great-great-grandmother.

Jenna granted your wish all right. She's sent you back to a time before you ever met her.

Way before.

And that was your last wish. So this story comes to an old-fashioned

END.

You clutch the can of cola tightly in your left hand. With your right, you quickly snap open the lid.

FFFFSSSZZZZZZZ!

With a fizzing, hissing sound, a huge cloud of vapor escapes from the can. It grows bigger and louder, filling the room. Then a frightening figure squeezes out of the can and floats in front of you.

"Jenna?" you gasp when you see her.

The genie hovers above you, a nasty grimace twisting her face. She looks so . . . different! Her hair is more spiky, and more colorful. Harsh red, glaring blue, angry green. Instead of a fuzzy sweater and jeans, she's wearing black leather from head to toe. The metal studs sticking out all over her jacket look as if they could cut you. The black leather pants are draped with heavy chains. Her huge black boots have sharp metal points on the toes.

Instead of greeting you with her cheery "What's up?," she growls. Or hisses. Like a cat. Her teeth are sharp and pointed too. She narrows her eyes and gives you a mean glare.

"So?" she snaps. "What do you *think* you want this time, smart-mouth?"

Answer her on PAGE 41.

You race to the water's edge, then start jogging along the beach to see where it leads.

You figure you'll eventually find a resort or something.

You spot footprints in the sand! Then you realize that they're yours! You've run in a big circle. You're back where you started. It's an island! A deserted island!

You flop down on the beach. And sit straight back up.

There's a rustling sound in the trees behind you. Maybe you're not as alone on this island as you thought.

Thick trees, hung with dense vines and brightly-colored flowers, crowd the middle of the island. It looks like a small, dark jungle.

"Hello?" you call out. "Anybody here?"

The trees stop rustling.

You listen hard, but the lapping of the waves makes it difficult to hear.

"Helllll-ooooo!" you shout, cupping your hands to your mouth.

Nothing.

And then you hear a roar. An animal roar!

If you look for a place to hide, turn to PAGE 72.

Or maybe you're better off staying where you are. You'd hate to get lost, or worse. If you stay put, turn to PAGE 65.

"I wish a monster would jump out of the closet and scare Randy — right now!" Kate says.

Oh, no, you think. Your stomach tightens into a million knots. You gaze at the closet door, which is still closed. Randy's friends are all laughing and making fun of Kate.

But when Randy's eyes meet yours, he realizes what you've already figured out.

Her wish is going to come true.

Any second now.

Turn to PAGE 43 — if you dare!

Are you sure you want to get rid of the huge monster insect? The monster that has your brother gripped in enormous claws?

You better believe it!

"Why not?" you demand. "Why shouldn't I wish the bug away?"

"Because your real mom is inside that cola can," Jenna whispers. "And if you don't find that can and wish her out of it, you'll never get rid of me."

"Can't *you* wish to switch places with my mom?" you ask hopefully.

Jenna shakes her head, rattling her earrings. "I don't get to make wishes myself," she explains. "I only grant them."

"Okay, okay." You try not to panic. "How about if *I* wish for her to come back — and for you to go away?"

"Couple of problems, kiddo." She snaps her gum at you. "One. You'd still have the bug on your hands. And two. I can't get back into the cola can if I don't have it!"

"Wish!" Randy screams as the bug pulls him closer. "Wish away the monster!"

What are you going to do?

If you use your last wish to get rid of the bug, turn to PAGE 115.

If you go to find the cola can first, turn to PAGE 119.

You can't make a wish without Jenna's cola can. And those three quarters were your only chance.

Even the parrot starts to cry!

You fling the cola can onto the ground in despair.

"No! No! No!" You slam your fist against the side of the cola machine.

Then something wonderful happens.

Another can of cola drops down.

"Can it be...?" You pick it up. "Oh, please, please, *please* be the right can!" You take a deep breath and flip open the top.

In a huge stinging spray of soda and red gas, Jenna shoots out of the can.

You hardly recognize her....

Her eyes are a poisonous yellow color, shaped like a cat's. Her teeth are *all* fangs now. Razor sharp and deadly. Her hair stands straight up in spiky points that look as deadly as her teeth.

"J-J-Jenna," you stammer. "What happened to you?"

Turn to PAGE 20.

You decide to ride the tiger.

It seems as if it's your only hope of catching up to Jenna.

You hurry back to the clearing. You crouch in some bushes and peer through the leaves at the tiger. He's still sitting there, not moving.

You can see his sharp teeth inside his open mouth as he pants.

Hmmmm.

Maybe you should sneak up on him, taking him by surprise.

You creep up behind the tiger. You reach out and grab a handful of the thick furry skin at his neck. Then, as quickly as you can, you straddle the animal like a horse.

The minute you climb onto him, he bolts up and sprints through the jungle.

"Help!" you scream, barely able to hang on.

The tiger's head whips around and he snarls ferociously in your face.

He looks as if he's going to snap your head off.

Turn to PAGE 133.

Your hands fly up to your face to protect it.

"AWWWRKKK!" the bird screams again.

Sharp claws dig into your skin as it lands on your shoulder!

"Aaaahhhhhhh!" you shriek, more in shock than in pain.

You turn your head slightly and peek out from behind your hands.

It's a parrot! You've got a great big parrot perched on your shoulder!

"Follow me," the parrot squawks. Then it reaches up with one clawed foot and pulls at your hair. "Follow me!" it screams.

Well?

Are you going to follow the parrot? If so, turn to PAGE 30.

If not, turn to PAGE 47.

You head for the pantry to check on James's progress. He should have found the genie by now!

As you cross through the family room, smoke begins pouring out of the pantry. But not smoke from a fire. Jenna's smoke!

Great! you think. That must mean James found the can with the genie in it. . . .

The smoky cloud grows bigger and bigger. You can't see. A whooshing sound fills your ears. You can't help coughing.

And then you realize something — this isn't Jenna's smoke. This is the cloud that appears when she grants a wish!

That's strange, you think. Why is the cloud here? I didn't make a wish.

As the smoke fades away, you discover that the family room has changed. All the video games and the huge-screen TV are gone. Instead, the walls are lined with floor-to-ceiling bookshelves — filled with old books!

You gaze around. You don't understand.

What happened?

Maybe you'll find out on PAGE 88.

30

The parrot removes its claw from your shoulder. Then it flies off, into the jungle.

You decide to follow it. Meeting a talking bird isn't any stranger than anything else that's happened to you today. And it might help you find the cola can. You never know.

Vines dangle in your face as you hurry to keep up with the colorful bird. It's way ahead of you, but it's easy to spot. Its brilliant yellow and blue feathers stand out in the dense green of the jungle.

Now that you're in it, the jungle seems huge. And confusing. With all the twists and turns you've taken, you don't think you'll ever find your way back out.

The bird leads you deeper and deeper into the jungle. Where could it be leading you?

Finally it lands on the top of a tall tree, a few feet ahead of you. It squawks again.

"Hurry up!" it calls in its scratchy parrot voice.

You pick up your pace.

Then you hear a low growl — from the bushes just ahead.

Is the parrot leading you into a trap?

Turn to PAGE 101.

"I wish to be a famous sports star," you tell Jenna.

"That's cool," Jenna says. She gives you a strange smile. "Yeah. *Very* cool."

An instant later, you hear a hissing sound.

Then the whole room fills up with a white cloud of smoke. You can't see a thing. When the cloud of smoke clears away, you find yourself standing outside in the middle of nowhere — on a frozen pond.

It's a crisp, clear, freezing cold winter day. All you can see for miles around is snow. Snow-covered trees. Snow-covered rocks. Snowy rolling hills. Even snow on the ice.

You glance down and realize that you're wearing skates — and holding a broom in your hands.

There's something heavy in your coat pocket.

"Hey!" you shout out. "Where am I?"

No one answers you.

"HEY! What happened?" you cry, beginning to panic. "Jenna? Where am I?"

No answer.

"Someone! Anyone! Where am I? Why didn't I get my wish?"

Turn to PAGE 37.

You decide to stay in the water.

Why not? you think. Maybe you'll be miraculously saved by some unseen force . . .

Yeah, right.

Maybe a whole bunch of paratroopers will drop out of the sky and land on the beach, bringing you knapsacks full of potato salad, fried chicken, peanut butter-and-jelly sandwiches, and candy bars.

In your dreams!

Somehow that's not quite what happens.

Instead, you simply burn to a crisp in the hot sun. The water you're splashing in acts like a giant mirror, reflecting the sun's intense light and heat back onto you.

Not a pretty sight, is it?

Of course not. In fact, you'd better close the book before things get really ugly.

Go on, close the book. This story's over.

Quick! Before the buzzards start circling . . .

THE END

What's Jenna doing? You tremble and swallow hard. You're terrified she's going to bite you with her razor-sharp teeth.

You gather up your courage and clear your throat. "Um, Jenna, didn't you tell me I had *three* wishes?"

Jenna snarls, baring her teeth again.

If she bites me, her teeth could tear my flesh to shreds, you think.

"Fine," Jenna snaps. "Wish away. If you think you can do any better this time!"

She's right. You don't want anything to go wrong with your wish. You have to phrase it very carefully. The problem was you weren't specific enough last time.

"I wish I were a famous baseball player," you finally say. Your voice is shaking, but you try to keep it steady so she won't notice how scared you are. "Can't you do that? I wish I were a famous baseball player — not this dumb curling thing!"

Jenna hisses like a cat. You skate a few feet backward. You wonder what she's going to do. Then she rolls her eyes. "Okay," she grumbles. "But remember. Now you've used up your second wish."

Turn to PAGE 68.

Your head hits the ground hard as you fall. For a minute, you actually see stars. You glance over at the tiger.

He's out cold!

Your heart sinks. You watch Jenna disappearing into the jungle.

Now I'll never catch her. Never!

Your head throbs from the fall. Your arms ache from holding on so tight. Your knees hurt from landing on them. Your whole body feels bruised.

You slump to the ground and just lie there, facedown in the dirt.

Slowly the truth dawns on you. You're never going to get off this island.

Jenna is too big. Too powerful.

And much too evil.

You can't possibly catch her. You can't outsmart her. And you'll never be able to steal her ring.

In frustration, you grab a handful of dirt and fling it into the air.

"It's not fair!" you cry.

That's when you see it. Something shiny — lying on the ground. Right beside the tiger's mouth!

Turn to PAGE 83.

"I *warned* you not to go outside," James scolds when you return. "Your parents will be very angry when they get back."

"Where are my parents, James?" you ask.

"They went to Honolulu for lunch on the family jet. But they'll be home soon. And this time I won't let you out of my sight."

Great. Just what you need. James hanging on your every move.

You wander around the mansion, bored. James follows you wherever you go. But even when you ask nicely, he refuses to leave you alone. And he won't play with you, either.

"I am a butler, not a playmate," he informs you.

How totally stupid is this? Your house is loaded with everything you've ever wanted. But you can't have any fun. You're a prisoner, trapped in your own house. And now you have James the watchdog, spying on you.

This wish isn't exactly working out the way you had planned.

Then you have an idea.

Find out what it is on PAGE 49.

The tiger is about to attack you? Oh, no!

"Yes," you tell Jenna quickly. "I wish the tiger would go away!"

Jenna snaps her fingers and there's a *POOF* of smoke behind you. You sigh. That must mean the tiger's gone. What a relief.

Then Jenna throws back her head and starts laughing. A horrible, evil, hideous laugh.

"Ha-ha-ha-ha!" she cries jubilantly. "Hee-hee-hee-hee-heh!"

You don't think her laughter is a very good sign.

"What's so funny?" you demand.

But Jenna is laughing too hard to answer.

"Come on, tell me," you beg. "What's the joke?"

"You are!" Jenna doubles over, cackling.

"Why? What do you mean?"

"You fool!" the parrot squawks. "If you had wished for your old life back, you would have been safe from the tiger anyway! You wasted your last wish!"

You smack your forehead. How could you have been so stupid?

You glare at Jenna. "You tricked me!" you cry angrily.

"All I did was grant your final wish," she replies, still smirking. "Now you must grant MINE!"

Turn to PAGE 118.

Stunned, you just stand on the ice in the freezing winter landscape, wondering what went wrong with your wish.

And what you should do now.

"Hello!" you cry one more time. "Anyone?"

"Quit yapping!" a voice behind you shouts.

You turn around and see a big, burly man in a heavy wool coat. He walks out of the snowy woods and steps onto the ice. You notice that he's wearing skates too. He's also carrying a broom.

With his shoulders hunched down, the huge man skates right toward you. He's holding the broom across his body with both hands — sort of like it's a weapon.

What's he going to do with that? you wonder.

For some reason, you feel almost certain he's going to smack you on the head.

"Help!" you cry, shivering from the freezing cold.

"Quit your whining!" the man yells. He has some kind of an accent. Maybe Scottish. He picks up speed. "Quit your whining or I'll give you something to whine about!"

The guy skates toward you with so much power and speed, you're afraid he's going to mow you down!

Turn to PAGE 54.

The cola can! You have to find it before someone else does.

Because who knows what would happen then?

Jenna warned you to be careful with it. It must be very special.

You spot a guy in an orange T-shirt hanging out near the television. He's holding an unopened can of cola, and talking to a bunch of Randy's friends.

Is that the one? Was that can sitting on the coffee table a minute ago?

You're just about to ask him, when you hear a sound you recognize all too well.

Your five-year-old sister, Kate.

Screaming her head off.

If you continue searching for the cola can, turn to PAGE 13.

If you run to see what's wrong with Kate, turn to PAGE 110.

You think hard, not wanting to make a choice too quickly.

Finally you decide. You've always wanted to be really good-looking. So cute that people would stop and stare at you.

"I wish to be good-looking," you tell the genie. "I want to be so stunning that people's mouths hang open when they see me."

Jenna giggles. "Yup!" she says, jumping up from the chair. "That's an easy one. I get it all the time."

That makes sense to you. You imagine a lot of people would want to be good-looking.

"Okay!" Jenna pops her gum. "Hold onto your socks, kiddo. Here goes!"

Turn to PAGE 71.

40

You decide to ignore Jenna's warning. You dash out of the bathroom. You push your way through the crowd of dancing, shouting kids who are spilling food and drinks all over the furniture.

Finally you reach the kitchen and find a can opener.

You set the cola can down on the counter.

Jenna races into the kitchen with tears in her eyes.

"Please don't," she begs. "*Please.* I'll do anything. You can eat dessert for breakfast. You can stay up till midnight every night of your life. Anything! Just *please* don't open that cola can."

"No way," you tell Jenna. "I'm going to get my mom out of here right now!"

Before she can stop you, you clamp the can opener onto the cola can. Then you turn the handle.

Go on to PAGE 123.

"Uh, I — I just w-w-want out of here," you stammer.

"*GRRRRR!*"

You stumble backward when Jenna growls at you. Why is she scaring you?

"I don't have all day," Jenna snarls, popping her bubble gum. "You want a wish? Make it."

All right, take it easy, you think. Just give me a chance.

But you're too nervous to think straight. You had a few good wishes planned out — until Jenna arrived. Now that she's being so mean to you, you can't remember any of them.

So you open your mouth and say the first thing that pops into your head.

"I wish I were somewhere else — far away from here," you blurt out.

Uh-oh. Are you sure that's the wish you wanted?

Get your wish on PAGE 12.

You gaze at the cola can.

"Why?" you ask Jenna.

"You'll find out," she answers mysteriously.

She looks so serious that you gently place the cola can back on the table.

Hey — didn't Jenna say she'd go back into the cola can each time you made a wish? So why is she still here?

Easy answer, you think. You *wished* it. You wished for her to be your mom. And it came true!

But if Jenna's out here, what's in the cola can now?

Randy stands up. You grab his arm. "Randy! She's not our real mom," you insist. "You've got to believe me!"

"Oh, stop already!" Randy yanks his arm away from you. "If she can grant wishes, I wish your face would turn blue."

He stomps out of the room. But at the doorway, he glances back at you.

"Yeow!" Randy shouts. "How did that happen?"

"What?" you ask.

"Your face," he cries, pointing. "It's . . . it's blue!"

You leap off the couch and race to a mirror.

Oh, no! Your face really is blue! Now what?

If you wish your face were its normal color again, turn to PAGE 53.

If you don't mind having a blue face, turn to PAGE 18.

The closet door flies open.

"Aaaaahhhhhh!" Kate screams, gripping your leg so hard you think your blood will stop flowing.

Inside the closet, flinging its arms and legs wildly, is a huge metallic creature. Its silver skull is enormous. A long gray tongue darts out at you between terrible silver teeth. The tongue makes a sickening sucking sound.

Randy's friends back away from the closet. They scream in such blood-curdling terror, you can't hear the band playing just a few feet away.

"What is it?" a girl screams.

"I don't know!" Randy shouts back.

Whatever it is, it looks hideous. And deadly.

You're doomed.

Turn to PAGE 74.

You stare at the bones, stunned. Too freaked out to move.

Then a tiny voice snaps you out of it.

"Get me out of here!"

You glance at the cola can on the kitchen counter. "Mom?" you ask. "Are you all right?"

You lift her gently from the can and set her on top of the toaster oven.

"Yes, I'm fine." She pats her hair. "But what's going on? Is your brother having a party? Make all those kids go home!"

She's bossing you around from the top of the toaster oven?

Yup! And you're going to obey her too. Because even though she's only five inches tall — she's still your mom! And now you're in *BIG* trouble.

THE END

"Well, I guess I want to be rich," you tell Jenna.

"Who wouldn't?" Jenna responds. Then she ducks her head. You can see she's trying to hide her laughter. "They all ask for that," she mutters. She fakes a yawn. "Bor-ing."

You feel your face flush. But you don't really care what she thinks. Now that you've decided on a wish, you want it to come true!

"So will you make me rich?" you demand.

"Okay, fine. No big deal," Jenna adds with a shrug. "But you have to say 'I wish I were rich' or else I can't deliver the goods. It's a primo genie rule."

You close your eyes and cross your fingers for good luck.

"I wish I were rich," you announce.

WHOOOOOOSH!

The room fills with a huge, white smoky cloud. You can't see a thing until . . .

Take a look on PAGE 135.

The monster insect's claw is about to close on you.

"Aaaahhh!" you scream in horror. "No!"

You grip the baseball bat tightly, swing your arms back, and let it fly.

WHAM! You smack the claw hard with the bat.

BAM! A second hit.

KA-SLAM! BAM! WHAM! Three more hard hits.

"Yiyyy!" you scream as the bat strikes one final time.

All at once, the giant claw pops open. It flies open wide, like a huge clam shell — revealing the horror of what's inside.

You gasp when you see it. Ten or fifteen smaller metallic claws — each one big enough to pinch your head off. Or crack your skull into a thousand little pieces, like a nutcracker.

The multiple claws spring out at you, snapping, snapping viciously.

"No!" you scream in utter terror.

All at once, you don't care what happens. You don't care whether you ever see your real mother again. All you want is for this monster to go away.

"I wish the monster would disappear forever!" you shriek.

Turn to PAGE 87.

You decide not to follow the parrot.

Wait a minute. Are you NUTS?

A *genie* in a *cola can* sends you to a deserted island. You don't have a prayer of ever getting home. Then, out of nowhere, a *parrot* lands on your shoulder and says, "*Follow me.*"

And you're *not* going to follow the parrot?

Do you *really* think that's the best choice?

Tell the truth — how many of these GIVE YOURSELF GOOSEBUMPS books have you read? Is this your first one?

If it is, you're excused. You obviously don't know how these things work, so we'll give you a break. Go back to the bottom of PAGE 28 and choose again.

But if you've ever read a GIVE YOURSELF GOOSEBUMPS book before this one — you should know better!

That parrot was obviously some sort of super-smart bird. Or maybe the genie in disguise. Or an escapee from a Florida theme park. Or maybe it worked for a secret government agency.

One way or another, that parrot was going to help you. You should have known that!

You also should have known that when you make a silly choice, you wind up on a page that has two words at the bottom:

THE END

You tiptoe along the polished marble hallway. This house is *huge*! You hope you don't get lost.

You gaze down an enormous stairway and spot the front door. You glance around quickly. Good — you're still alone. You dart down the stairs and out through the double oak doors.

Outside, you wander over to the ten-car garage where the driver is polishing a new Rolls Royce. You wonder if he has the same orders as the butler.

Only one way to find out!

Ask him on PAGE 137.

"That's it!" you cry. "The answer!"

"What is it?" James asks. He raises an eyebrow.

You ignore his question. You're too busy figuring out a plan. *Yes!* You'll fix everything with another wish!

Now all you have to do is find that cola can.

"James!" You smile at the butler. "Do we have any cola?"

"There are forty cases of cola in the pantry. Shall I get you a can?"

Forty cases? Uh-oh. Which can has the genie in it?

If you open every can until you find the genie, turn to PAGE 59.

If you order James to do it for you and go check out the big-screen TV instead, turn to PAGE 8.

50

Those angry parents seem ready to tear *your* head off! And they're coming closer.

"I'm sorry," you try to explain. "But it was so hot and — "

All at once, the group of grown-ups rushes straight at you!

Yikes! You whirl around and run through the studio.

"Grab Wilfred! Grab Wilfred!" the parents chant.

They chase you through the dark backstage area and then down the maze of hallways leading to your dressing room.

You spot your dressing-room door. You reach out for the doorknob when a mother with long red fingernails grabs your costume.

"Got him!" she cheers. You hear a ripping sound as you wriggle out of her grip. You yank open the door to the dressing room and slam it shut. Luckily, it has a lock.

Outside, the angry parents pound on your door, shouting at you. "Come out of there! We're going to give you what you deserve!"

Inside, you close your eyes and quickly make another wish.

But you're so hot — and nervous — you can't think. So you just wish for the first thing that comes into your head.

Turn to PAGE 77.

How do you say "tough luck" to your mom?

"Uh, Mom," you begin. "Uh, I can't get you out of there."

"What?" your mom shrieks. "Why not?"

"A genie gave me three wishes and I've already used two," you explain. "So I'd have to use up my last wish to get you out."

"Hmmmmmmm." Your mother puts a tiny finger on the tip of her nose. That's what she always does when she's thinking.

Then she gestures for you to bring your face down to the can. She whispers in your ear. You have to strain to hear her.

"Mom!" you cry. "You're a genius!"

Then you turn to Jenna. "Here's my wish," you tell the genie. "I wish for unlimited wishes!"

"No! No! No!" Jenna flops down on the floor, kicking and screaming. "I hate that wish!"

You cross your arms and glare at her. "Well, that's the wish! You have to give it to me."

"Okay," Jenna grumbles. She snaps her fingers. "Satisfied?"

You and your mom grin at each other. She reaches her hand out of the can to slap you a high five. You tap her palm with your pinkie.

From now on, you're going to listen to your mom! She's pretty cool after all!

THE END

Your leg hurts, but it doesn't slow you down much. You run back into the street to escape the rat-man.

And right into a fight.

The ninja men followed you here. They have Stephanie cornered. When they notice you, they just laugh.

"Steph! Let's move!" you shout.

But it's no use. As soon as you turn to dart away, another Mortal Revenge villain appears out of nowhere, blocking your path. He's wearing a leather jacket. A ski mask covers his face.

You freeze. Three martial arts experts behind you. One in front of you. Are you doomed?

Your new attacker rips off the ski mask. You gasp.

It's Jenna!

"You have one wish left," Jenna informs you with an evil glare. "And let me tell you what it is. You wish that I weren't a genie. You wish I were an ordinary person with no magical powers. Now say it! Say that's your wish — and set me free!"

You take a step backward.

And feel the hot breath of a Mortal Revenge ninja on your neck.

Turn to PAGE 70.

Your face really is blue! Bright blue. Even your scalp is blue. You rub at the color, hoping it will come off. No luck. You are permanently blue — but just down to your neck. The rest of you is the regular color.

"What's going on?" you cry, whirling around to face Jenna.

"He made a wish — I granted it," she says with a shrug. "I'm the mom. And I say everyone in this family gets two more wishes. Like you've got two more wishes. You got a problem with that?"

"Yes, I've got a problem!" you scream at her. "Look at me!"

"You don't like it," Jenna snaps, "fix it."

You hate to use up your second wish this way. But you've got to. You can't stand to go around with a blue face!

"Okay, okay," you mutter. "I wish my face were the normal color again."

You run back to the mirror to see if the wish worked. But you can already tell from Randy's reaction — it did.

"Wow!" he says to Jenna. "Awesome! How did you do that, Mom?"

"It's easy," Jenna brags. "I've had years of practice. *Thousands* of years."

Randy glances at you with a twinkle in his eye.

"I know what I want next!" he announces.

"Randy — don't you dare!" you scream at him.

Turn to PAGE 98.

There's no point in trying to out-skate the burly man. Where would you go? You don't know where you are. He may be your only hope.

You wince as he reaches you at top speed. But he skids to a quick stop just in time. "What's the matter, champ?" he says. "Why are you just standing there, complaining?"

You figure you have a lot to complain about — no wish, no way to get home. But you can't explain that to this stranger.

He'd never believe you.

What happened? you wonder. Didn't the genie understand your wish? Didn't she know you wanted to be a famous sports star?

Where's the stadium? The locker room? The fans?

"Come on, champ." The guy claps you on your shoulder. "Just because you're the best curler in all of Canada doesn't mean you don't have to practice, you know. Got to get busy for the World Curling Championships, don't we?"

"Huh?" You have no idea what this guy is talking about. "What's curling?"

The burly man throws back his head and laughs. "What's curling?" he shouts, still roaring with laughter. "That's a fine question from the captain of the world's best curling team!"

Turn to PAGE 75.

Your eyes focus in on the cola can in Murphy's hand. He's clutching it as if it's made of solid gold. Not drinking it. Just holding it. And standing next to his Ferrari.

It's YOUR cola can! You just know it.

"Hey!" you call from the convertible. "That's my cola can!"

But the minute Murphy sees you coming, he hops in the Ferrari and speeds off.

Looks like your wishes just hit the road. And unless you want to squeeze back into that pink-and-green dragon costume — maybe you'd better do the same thing!

THE END

56

You stare into the dark dressing-room closet.

Something green-and-pink stares back at you.

A green and pink *Wilfred* costume!

Not Wilfred! You *hate* Wilfred! Wilfred is the worst TV character ever invented. He's a huge green-and-pink talking dragon — the star of a stupid preschoolers' TV show.

What's that doing in there? you wonder. I never wished for a Wilfred costume!

A sharp knock interrupts your thoughts. The door swings open. A pretty blond woman clutching a clipboard steps into the room.

"Time to get into your costume, Wilfred, babe," she tells you. "We've got a live audience of four-year-olds. And they're just dying to get their peanut-butter-and-jelly-smeared hands all over you!"

You shake your head in horror. No! It can't be. You're not Wilfred — are you?

"Me?" you ask.

"Who else?" the young woman asks. "You're the star."

Well, Wilfred, babe. It's show time! What do you say?

If you try being Wilfred for awhile, turn to PAGE 19.

If you get out of there right now by making another wish, turn to PAGE 63.

Peter continues staring at the money you gave him as he follows you toward the Rolls Royce.

"What's the matter?" you tease. "Haven't you ever seen a hundred-dollar-bill before? I've got plenty more!"

You toss some hundred-dollar-bills in the air, then climb into the car. Peter scrambles in after you. As you drive away, you glance back. Several neighbors are snatching the bills off the ground.

"You have to be more careful," Manny scolds from the front seat. "Money can make people act crazy."

"Manny, you worry too much." You stretch out against the roomy back seat. "From now on, we're going to have fun."

You and Peter help yourselves to sodas and snacks from the mini-bar. "First, we're going to replace our old sneakers with high-tech models," you explain to Peter on the way to the mall.

"Next, we're going to see all the movies at the twelve-plex. Then we'll head over to the food court and eat one of everything!"

"Mmmph!" Peter nods happily, his mouth full of corn chips.

As Manny guides the Rolls into a parking spot, a crowd gathers. They seem to be talking about the car.

Find out what they're saying on PAGE 108.

58

You jump, startled by Jenna's anger.

"What's wrong?" you ask her. "Why shouldn't I use a can opener on the can?"

"You just can't," Jenna says firmly. "No way. That's *my* can. I decide what happens to it."

"But my mom's in there," you protest.

Jenna drags you out of the family room, to a bathroom down the hall. It's quieter in there. More private.

"Take my word for it — that's not the way to get her out," Jenna insists. Her eyes flash a scary warning look at you.

"Who are you talking to?" your tiny mother calls from inside the can. She's so small, almost everything she says sounds like a whine. "Are you going to get me out or not?"

Well? Are you?

For an instant, you're not sure what to do.

Your mom sounds so pathetic. You really want to help her.

And besides, you're getting sick of having Jenna around.

But you don't want to use up your last wish to get your mom out of the can. So what are you going to do?

If you open the can with a can opener, turn to PAGE 40.

If you tell your mom "tough luck," turn to PAGE 51.

"Uh, no thank you, James," you tell the butler. "I'll get the cola myself. Just tell me where it is."

A few minutes later, you're sitting in the pantry, surrounded by forty cases of cola. James posts himself right outside.

It's going to be a big job to open all of these cans.

FSST! POP. FSST. FSST. POP. FSST . . .

Your finger begins to hurt from prying up all those little metal fliptops. You open the cans faster and faster.

FSST. PSSST. POP. FSST. FSST. FSST . . .
FSSSZZZZRRRRRRT!

"WHOA!" you cry as blue gas sprays from the can. You drop the can to the floor.

You watch in amazement as the can spins around on the floor, vibrating and humming. The blue gas continues to pour out.

Blue gas? What's going on? It wasn't blue before, and it didn't shoot out of the can with such force.

You're struck by the horrible feeling that something very different is happening this time.

The hissing sound grows louder and louder. Then you fling your arms over your face as the can explodes! Shards of metal fly through the air, and something huge bursts out of the can!

Turn to PAGE 78.

"We've got to do something!" Randy shouts.

No kidding!

The enormous metal monster crawls further into the room. Its antennae wave as if it's searching for prey. Then its head slowly turns your way. It seems to have found what it was looking for.

You!

You feel along the wall, desperate to find a weapon — anything you can use to defend yourself.

Your fingers touch a baseball bat leaning against the doorway. Luckily, Randy never puts his things away.

The monster creeps closer . . . closer. . . .

If you bash the giant insect with the baseball bat, turn to PAGE 46.

If you try to escape by running outside, turn to PAGE 129.

"Let's pick up Stephanie," you tell Manny. "We can play video games back at the house."

"So it's true," Stephanie exclaims when she climbs into the car. "You're a millionaire! How did it happen?"

"Just lucky I guess." You don't tell Stephanie about the genie granting your wish to be rich. She'd never believe you!

When you arrive back at your mansion, the two of you grab a tray of sodas and snacks and head into the family room. You wave at the entertainment centers lining the walls. "What do you want to play?"

Stephanie picks up the video game controller. "Mortal Revenge," she announces. "If you dare!"

You pop the Mortal Revenge video game into the machine. It's one of your favorites too. Pretty soon, you and Stephanie are karate-kicking your way through a street gang of bad guys.

"Great shot, Steph!" you cheer. "You're good at this." You grab a can of cola. All this action is making you thirsty.

"Thanks! Mortal Revenge is the coolest." Stephanie keeps her eyes focused on the screen. "I wish it were real!"

"Me too." You flip open the can of soda. "I wish we were doing this in real life."

With a hiss, white smoke fills the room.

What's happening? Turn to PAGE 69 to find out.

"No way," you tell Jenna. "I'm not falling for your tricks anymore. I just want my old life back. Just like I said."

Jenna's face twists into an awful, ugly shape. "Are you *sure*?"

"Yes," you answer firmly. "That's my wish. Give it to me."

"Fine!" Jenna snaps. She puts her hands on her hips and glares at you.

"Come on!" you order her. "Give me my wish!"

A huge smile spreads across her face — although she's so ugly, it doesn't look like a smile. It looks like an alligator's hideous snarl.

"Oooops," she says with a giggle. "I forgot to tell you. The third wish is different."

"What?" You stare at her. "Different how?"

"Before I grant your last wish," she explains, "you have to steal this wish-ring from my finger!" She waggles her pinkie at you. Wrapped around it is an enormous ruby ring.

Turn to PAGE 76.

Forget it, you decide. You do not want to be Wilfred. Even if he is a big star.

Why would you? That creep? That sickeningly cutesy dragon with the singsong theme song and the goody-goody slogan — "A Wilfred Hug makes the world safe and snug?"

No way. You are not going on that TV show! So you close your eyes and make another wish.

Turn to PAGE 77.

That hot-dog counter looks like a perfect hiding place. If you can reach it, you might be safe there until things calm down.

You and Peter crawl as fast as you can under the food court tables. Your knees feel bruised and your hands are sticky from the spilled food on the floor. But you reach the booth unnoticed.

Quickly, you jump up and leap over the counter. *BRINGGG! BRINGGG! BRINGGG!*

A blaring siren blasts your ears.

"Oh no!" you cry. "What's that?"

Lights start flashing as the siren shrieks louder and louder.

"All right, all right, break it up!" you hear someone order.

It's the mall police! Now you're in trouble!

In fact, you're in BIG trouble. Breaking and entering is a serious crime. They thought you were trying to rob the place.

You try to tell them you're the richest kid in the world. That you could *buy* that hot-dog shop. That you could buy the whole mall!

Too bad they don't buy your story. So for you it's bye-bye.

THE END

At least on the beach, you have a clear view all around you. You have a better chance of escaping from something in the open.

And besides, you reassure yourself, if something horrible happens, you still have one more wish left. You can still use it to save yourself.

Well, if you're stuck on a deserted island, you might as well try to enjoy yourself. You run down to the water and splash around in the waves for a while.

The water is bright clear blue. Cool but not cold. Beautiful orange-and-black striped fish dart away from your feet.

Everything would be perfect. Except for the rustling and the roaring sound coming from the jungle. That keeps moving closer.

Pretty soon, you realize that you're dying of thirst. But now you're afraid to come out of the water. Afraid of the beast in the jungle.

And as far as you can see, there's not a thing to drink in sight. No fresh babbling brook. No cooler full of lemonade. No cola machines . . .

"Hold it a minute!" you sputter, realizing something.

Cola! Where's the can of cola with the genie in it?

"Without that can, I'll *never* get off this island!" you moan.

Go on to PAGE 91.

66

For a minute, you don't know what to say.

This totally cool genie pops out of a cola can and offers you three wishes? You can't believe it!

But you know what you'll wish for. Something awesome. You can picture it there in front of you.

Before you put it into words, you hear a car pull up.

"Uh, oh," you tell the genie quickly. "My mom's home. You've got to hide! Come on. To my room!"

Motioning for her to follow you, you race down the hall. You push Jenna behind your closet door, so your mom won't see her when she comes in.

And you *know* your mom will come in any minute now. She always does. First thing, every day when you get home from school, she nags you about your homework. Then scolds you about not making your bed. And then insists you clean your room.

"Hi, Lambikins!" your mom calls as she enters the house.

You cringe when you hear the babyish name.

Jenna snorts. Then she pretends to put a finger down her throat and fakes a gag.

You giggle. "You're so cool. I wish *you* were my mom," you blurt out.

"You wish I were your mom?" Jenna declares. "I can do that."

Uh-oh. You've just made your first wish! Turn to PAGE 136.

You swallow hard, trying to make the lump in your throat go away. But it won't. You're too choked with fear.

Still, you decide to do what the parrot says. It got you this far. You figure it must know what it's talking about.

You ignore the tiger. Or at least you try. You can't completely forget about the ferocious beast. You're only human.

"N-n-now what?" you ask the parrot, still shaking. You try holding very still, so as not to attract the tiger's attention. "H-how do I get the can of cola? I haven't got any money."

"Take these quarters," the parrot answers. Using its claw, it picks up three quarters from the branch it's perched on, and offers them to you. "But be careful. They're the only ones I have left."

As you reach out to take the quarters, the tiger LEAPS! Six-hundred pounds of hungry snarling animal — right toward you!

Maybe you shouldn't have listened to that crazy old bird!

Don't move a muscle until you get to PAGE 15!

POOF! In a cloud of white smoke, the genie grants your wish and disappears.

When the smoke clears, a familiar sound fills your ears.

"YEEAAAAHHHHH!" a crowd roars.

You open your eyes, and glance around.

Fantastic! This is more like it!

You're in Yankee Stadium, stepping up to the plate with a crowd of thousands cheering and calling your name. Your nickname, that is. They're calling you the "Great One!"

"Great One! Great One! Great One!" they chant in rhythm.

That is so cool! you think. I must be awesome.

And you are. You hit three home runs that game alone. Your dream has come true!

In fact, you're so happy with your new life that you never want to change a thing. Ever. So you never use your last wish.

Then one day, when you're signing autographs after a World Series game, a kid comes up to you and says, "Great One, I wish I could have something of yours. Please? Just anything."

So you reach into your gym bag and pull out the old cola can. The one with the genie inside. You toss the can to the kid.

"Sometimes wishes *do* come true!" you say as you stroll away.

THE END

The smoky white gas chokes you, making it impossible to breathe. Your heart pounds as you realize what is happening.

You accidentally made a wish!

You popped open the cola can — the one with the genie in it. Then you said, "I wish we were doing this in real life."

Bad move.

Because when the smoke clears, you find yourself standing in the middle of a dark alleyway — facing three guys dressed from head to toe in black silk. Horrible masks cover their faces. They look just like the ninjas in Mortal Revenge.

Except that they're real!

Terrifyingly real.

And they're heading straight toward you and Stephanie!

Turn to PAGE 99.

You realize you're trembling. Jenna's eyes glow with hate.

"Okay," you mutter. There goes your final wish. But you have no choice.

Jenna hurls a cola can at you. "Do the deed," she snarls.

You yank the can's flip top. "I wish . . . " you mumble.

"Say it so I can hear you!" Jenna shrieks. The Mortal Revenge guys circle you and Stephanie. You are surrounded.

"I wish you weren't a genie," you say. "I wish you were an ordinary person with no magical powers."

The cola can shakes in your hand. It gets hot — so hot that you drop it to the ground. Instead of being blinded by white misty smoke, everything goes black. A blackness filled with a horrible sound — the sound of Jenna's terrifying, screaming laughter.

Finally the blackness fades away. The shrieking stops. Slowly, you open your eyes.

You're home! Your old home! No mansion! No multiple entertainment centers! Just you and Stephanie playing a regular video game. On an ordinary TV.

"What happened?" Stephanie asks. "That game seemed so real."

"Yeah," you agree. "Too real. But I have a feeling we won in

THE END."

WHOOOOSH!

White smoke fills the room. It smothers you —
but only for a second. Then it clears as quickly as
it came.

You can't wait to look in the mirror!

Except that you can't move! Not an inch! Something's holding you in place! As if you're frozen in
ice!

A horrible tight feeling of fear grips your
throat, closing it so tight, you can't even swallow.

What's happening? You try to speak, to scream
for help, but you can't open your mouth.

Oh, no! You're paralyzed!

What did the genie do?

*Since you can't move, ask someone to turn the
pages for you. Go to PAGE 112.*

You've got to hide, you decide.

Somewhere where you'll be safe from that beast, that thing — whatever it was — that roared.

But where?

You gaze around at the beach and beyond it. Except for the jungle — and you certainly can't go in there! — there's only one good hiding place.

A cave.

A small cave. An opening in some rocks near the water.

You hadn't spotted it before. But now it seems like the perfect hiding place.

You hear the roar again. Louder this time. It is definitely moving closer.

With one eye on the jungle, you slink toward the rocks. Toward that safe, dark opening.

Your heart pounds.

What if the beast is watching you? What if he sees you going into the cave, and follows you in there?

Then you'll be trapped . . .

As you reach the cave, you heart starts to beat a little faster. You aren't sure if you really want to go in. You peer inside. From deep in the darkness, six pairs of eyes stare back!

Find out what's in the cave on PAGE 89.

"Uh, I guess I want to be famous," you tell Jenna.

"That's cool." Jenna smiles. She jumps up from the chair and paces around your family room. "I can picture it. You're huge. You're recognized wherever you go. Your face is on every magazine cover in the universe!"

Then she stops in the middle of the room and stares at you. She's chewing bubble gum, and she blows a big bubble.

"But like, what kind of famous?" she asks you. "I mean, do you want the major celebrity-movie-star-TV thing? Or how about a famous sports star? Or what?"

"Any of that stuff would be great," you reply quickly.

"Well, it's your wish, kiddo." She snaps her bubble gum in your face. "Pick."

Want to be a famous movie-TV star? Turn to PAGE 85.

Want to be a famous sports star? Turn to PAGE 31.

"Helllllp!" Kate screams over and over again. "Helllpppp!"

You want to help, but you're frozen in terror. Your eyes are glued to the monster. Its arms and legs flail, desperately trying to escape from the closet.

Kate bolts out of the room. Randy's friends follow, stumbling and screaming.

Still you can't move. You can't tear your eyes away. The metallic monster's antennae waggle at you. Big drops of saliva roll off its tongue and splat on to the floor.

"Gross," Randy moans. "Quick! Wish it away!"

"You wish it away!" you snap. You've only got one wish left. You have to use it carefully.

"I can't!" Randy shrieks. "I've used mine up!"

CRAASHHH!

Suddenly, the giant metallic insect punches one long, wiry leg through the wall. A sharp pincer-claw on the end of its leg reaches out toward Randy. It grabs his arm!

"What are you waiting for?" Randy screams. "Wish it away!"

"No — wait!" Jenna suddenly rushes up to you. "Are you sure you want to do that?"

Turn to PAGE 25.

"Come on, what's curling?" you ask again.

But he just laughs and shakes his head.

Finally you face the facts. He thinks you're just joking. He's not going to answer.

A few minutes later, some other curlers show up. You watch them, and figure out what the sport is.

Curling is a game where teams of four people try to slide a heavy stone over the ice, toward a circle — using brooms to sweep the ice in front of the stone!

"I don't believe this," you mutter to yourself.

Not only are the rules weird, it seems to only be played by people your grandfather's age!

What am I doing here? you think to yourself.

But the real question is, what are you going to do now?

One thing's for sure. You need to be more careful how you word your wishes.

If you want to try a totally new wish, turn back to PAGE 5. Choose again from the wishes at the bottom of the page.

If you still want to be a famous sports star — but you want to pick the sport yourself — turn to PAGE 80.

Steal her pinkie ring?

"But . . . but . . . that's not fair!" you cry.

"Who said anything about fair?" Jenna laughs. "And to get the ring, you're going to have to catch me first!"

Then she snaps her fingers. She disappears into a cloud of smoke. Once the smoke clears, you sink to the ground in horror.

Jenna — the new ugly, monstrous, hideous, mean Jenna — has grown four times her normal size!

You lean your head back. Your eyes travel up, up, up her enormous body. She's grown as big as a small building. She could squash you like a bug, just by moving one foot.

"So long, kid," she booms. "I wouldn't count on getting that last wish, if I were you!"

Jenna turns and starts strolling through the jungle. With every step, she tramples several small trees. Her legs are so long, each stride takes her farther and farther away.

I'll never catch her, you think, as she leaves you hopelessly behind.

Turn to PAGE 130.

"I wish I were far away from here," you murmur. "Anywhere but here."

Nothing happens.

"Come on, Jenna!" you whisper. "Where are you?" You look up at the ceiling. Glance at the corners. You gaze all around the dressing room. "Oh, Jenna," you call.

Nothing.

Did she lie to me about giving me three wishes? you wonder. Am I going to be stuck as Wilfred forever?

Then you remember. The cola can!

Jenna *warned* you. There's no way to make a wish without that can!

You think hard, trying to remember. Where was the can last time you had it? You close your eyes, trying to picture it.

Let's see . . . Jenna was pacing the room and —

You snap your fingers. That's it! The cola can was on the coffee table in your family room.

Then you made your wish and . . . *POOF!*

You were here. Now the question is, did the can travel with you when your wish came true? Is it hidden in your dressing room somewhere? Or is it back where you left it? In your family room.

If you think the can is still back at your house, turn to PAGE 103.

If you think it's in the dressing room somewhere, turn to PAGE 82.

Amazingly, you survive the explosion with only a scratch on your arm.

The blue mist completely fills the room now. And floating inside the cloud is a terrifying sight.

A genie. And it's not Jenna. No, it's a very different genie.

A fat, monstrous-looking man, in a gold satin shirt and black metallic pants, hovers above you. Green warts cover his leathery face and hands, making him look like a toad. He must be about seven feet tall.

"You rang?" he snarls, as he floats before you in mid-air.

"No!" you cry out nervously. "I mean, maybe. Where's Jenna? What's going on?"

"Jenna called in sick," the warty guy growls. "I'm filling in for her. My name is Toobah." He floats over to you and breathes hard in your face.

Ewwwww. Your nose wrinkles at the smell of his breath. It's sour, like bad milk.

"You've got two wishes left." His voice booms at you from above. "And if you're smart, you'll use one of them to wish you'd never met me!"

If you take your chances with Toobah, turn to PAGE 100.

If you take his advice and wish you'd never met him, turn to PAGE 122.

"Hey, Randy," Jenna answers. She's chewing gum and popping it loudly. "Good day at school?"

"It was okay," Randy answers her. "But I got kicked out of math class — for not having my homework done."

Jenna shakes her head. "Your teacher's a jerk," she tells Randy. "Don't worry about it."

"Right," Randy agrees. He flops down on the couch beside her.

You stare at him, your eyes wide. Then you stare at Jenna. You can't believe this.

A totally cool version.

Why does Randy act as if he knows her? As if he's seen her before? Why isn't he freaking out?

"What are *you* looking at, goof?" Randy snaps at you.

"Uh, Rando," you say, using his nickname. You lower your voice and lean close to him. "See that person next to you? With all the earrings and the combat boots and the wild hair? Who is it?" you ask him.

"What planet are *you* on?" Randy snorts. "That's Mom."

Go on to PAGE 90.

This curling game may be a load of fun for these old guys, but it wasn't what you had in mind when you made your wish!

There must be some way to fix this wish, you think. But how?

You shove your freezing hands deep into your pockets. Your fingers hit a heavy object. From the weight of it, it seems as if it might be a cola can. You pull it out.

YES! It is! The genie must have put it there when you made your first wish.

You turn away from the other curlers, and skate to the edge of the pond.

Then you hold the cola can in your hands and flip open the top.

Turn to PAGE 14.

"Let's go to Sal's Sports Spa," you suggest. "The new PowerPlay shoes are in."

"Sounds good to me!" Peter replies.

At Sal's, you and Peter try on the high-tech sneakers. Then you try on hockey skates, soccer shoes, and climbing boots.

"Peter! Look at these!" You hold up a pair of motorized in-line skates. "I'd like to try these on next," you instruct the frazzled clerk.

She glares at you. "Quit wasting my time," she snaps. "I need to pay attention to *real* customers!"

"But we *are* real customers!" you explain.

The clerk raises an eyebrow. "Kid, do you have any idea how much these things cost? Your allowance might cover the laces."

Obviously, she doesn't realize who you are. You pull out your wallet. Several hundred-dollar-bills fall out of your pockets and float to the floor. The clerk's eyes widen.

"I want to buy all the shoes we've tried on," you announce. "*And* I'm buying shoes for everyone in the store!"

"Hey!" you hear someone shout. "There's a kid buying shoes for everybody!"

Yikes! Dozens of customers rush into the store all at once. It looks like you're going to be trampled!

Look for a place to hide on PAGE 127!

You decide to search for the cola can in the dressing room. It's got to be around here somewhere!

You start searching the drawers and closets. Yanking open one after another. No luck.

Finally you notice a small, wood-paneled cabinet in the corner of the room. It's the right shape and size to be a mini-refrigerator. You dash over and flip open the door.

YES! It's filled with bottles of juice, bottles of sparkling water — and cans of cola! Just what you're looking for.

You pull out a cola can and flip open the top.

SSSZZZTT! The soda sprays you lightly in the face. It's just a soft drink. No genie.

You grab another can, then another one. *SSSZZZTT! SSSZZZTT!*

More carbonated beverage hits you in the face. No Jenna.

There's only one can of cola left in the back of the mini-fridge. What are the chances? Your heart starts to sink.

Turn to PAGE 22.

Scrambling madly, you reach out and pick up the small, shiny object.

"Yes!" you shout when you see what it is.

The genie's ring! Your mind races back until you figure it out. It must have flown off her hand when she smacked the tiger. Then it must have gotten small again somehow. When it fell to the ground, away from Jenna's magic.

You squeeze the ring tightly in both hands and close your eyes.

"I wish I could go home," you whisper. "I want to go back to the way it was before I met Jenna. Except I want to remember everything that's happened to me."

All at once, the earth shakes. A terrifying pounding sound fills your ears.

It's Jenna! you realize with a gulp. Marching toward you.

BOOM! BOOM! BOOM!

Branches break and leaves are ripped to shreds as the giant genie moves in your direction.

Finally she bursts through the trees. Her eyes are wild, her fangs sharp enough to rip you to shreds.

Don't make a move — just turn to PAGE 92.

"Aaaaahhhhhhhhhh!"

You let out a scream as the rat-man leaps at you, swords swirling. You dive out of the way, toward the pile of bricks.

Ooof! Pain shoots up your leg as you fall to the floor. The rat-man is right behind you. He drops his sword and grabs at you with his four arms, sinking his teeth into your shin.

"Get off!" you shriek. You kick at him with your other leg. "Oww! Noooo!"

You kick his snout over and over, but he's too strong. You reach your arm out and manage to grab one of the bricks lying nearby. You bring it down hard, right on the rat's snout.

With a howl of pain, the rat-man instantly releases you and leaps to his feet. You scurry behind the pile of bricks.

The rat-man snatches up the samurai swords again.

And heads your way.

Run back to PAGE 9.

A movie star, you decide. Or TV star. It doesn't matter.

"Okay, so say it," Jenna demands, still snapping her bubble gum at you. "I can't give you your wish until you talk the talk. Say the words. Genie rules. Got it?"

"Oh, sure," you answer. "Okay. Uh . . ."

You close your eyes. Out of habit. You always close your eyes when you make a wish.

"I wish I were a famous TV star," you mumble softly.

WHOOSH.

You hear a hissing sound, then feel a burst of steam or smoke or something. When you open your eyes, you find that the whole room is filling up with a white cloud.

You can't see a thing.

And you start to cough. You can't breathe! It's the smoke. It's filling your lungs! It's going to smother you!

She tricked me, you think, as you struggle and gasp for air.

The genie tricked me!

Turn to PAGE 120.

"Help me!" a tiny voice begs from inside the soda can. "Get me out of here — right now!"

Your heart skips a beat as you peer into the can. You gasp.

Inside the can is a tiny living person with blond hair and pink sweatpants.

It's your mom! Except that she's only five inches tall!

"Mom?" you shriek.

"Get me out of here!" your mother calls from inside the can. "I'm trapped!"

You glance around the dark family room to see if anyone's watching. No one is. The music is blaring so loudly, no one else seems to hear your mom talking inside the can.

"Get me out," your mom cries, "or you're going to be in big trouble!"

You don't know whether to laugh or cry. Your mom has shrunk to the size of a pencil, but she's still scolding you.

"Okay," you assure your mom. "I'll get you out."

But how? She's too big to fit through the hole. And you really don't want to use up your last wish getting her out. "Should I use a can opener?" you wonder out loud.

Suddenly someone grabs your arm.

"NO!" Jenna shouts in your ear.

Turn to PAGE 58.

WHOOOSH!

An instant of pure darkness. Then silence.

The whole world seems to come to a stop.

Did the earth stop spinning? Did the stars go out?

Finally, you can see again. You open your eyes. You glance at Randy, who has collapsed on the floor. He gives you a weak smile and a thumbs-up.

You sigh with relief.

The huge metallic insect is gone. . . .

You creep over to the window and peek out.

No monster out there.

Did it work? Is it really gone?

Turn to PAGE 16.

You try to figure out what just happened. Your eyes search the family room for clues. You spot James. He must have snuck out of the pantry in the smoke. He's lounging in a big leather chair, wearing a velvet robe and reading the newspaper.

He snaps his fingers. "You there," he calls. "Bring me a glass of iced tea."

What's going on here? you wonder. Then you glance down at your clothes. You aren't wearing jeans anymore.

You're wearing black pants, a white jacket, and white gloves. There's a silver tray in your hand.

The truth hits you quickly, like a kick in the stomach.

James finally found the right can of cola, and Jenna popped out. Then he must have made his own wish and switched places with you! You're *his* servant now.

"Oh," James adds. "Don't get any ideas about hunting around for that cola can with the delightful young lady inside. I've hidden it nicely." He laughs. A not-very-nice laugh.

Oh, well, you think, as you trudge to the kitchen. You have to serve James because you were too lazy to open all those cola cans yourself. Looks as if it *serves* you right!

THE END

Bats! you think.

Those six pairs of eyes, glowing in the darkness, must be bats.

Except that they're too big for bats. Bats have tiny little eyes. These eyes look like they belong to . . .

To what? Bears? Wolves?

You freeze. Terrified. You want to turn and run, but you don't dare move. What if the six pairs of eyes suddenly attack?

And besides . . .

If you go out, you'll have to face the beast in the jungle. And the growling is getting louder . . .

Suddenly, from deep in the cave, you hear breathing.

Then movement. The eyes are coming toward you!

Turn to PAGE 125.

This is getting weird. Way too weird.

She's really done it! Jenna has turned into your mom!

You're not at all sure you like it. . . .

"Rando." You try again. "That's not really Mom. Our mom is blond, and she's forty years old, and she wears pink sweatpants. Remember?"

"Give me a break!" Randy punches you lightly on the shoulder. "I'm not in the mood for games."

"I'm serious!" you whisper loudly. "That's not Mom! That's some kind of genie who just came out of a cola can. She gave me three wishes, and I wished she'd be our mom. And now she is."

"Very funny," Randy says. But he doesn't laugh.

"I'll prove it to you," you tell him.

You reach over and grab the cola can sitting on the coffee table in front of him. It's the can you just opened — the can Jenna popped out of. But it's not open anymore.

You stare down at it. How can this be? you wonder. The can is sealed up and it feels full.

"Hey — careful with that," Jenna warns.

Turn to PAGE 42.

The cola can! Where is the cola can?

As if in answer to your silent question, roars come echoing out of the jungle again.

It sounds as if the beast has moved to the trees at the very edge of the beach. What kind of beast is it? you wonder.

Your heart starts to pound wildly. Your blood pumps so hard in your veins, you can feel it throbbing in your neck.

You've got to find that cola can!

"What am I supposed to do now?" you whisper.

Talking to yourself out loud makes you feel a little less scared. So you decide to keep it up.

"Think, stupid," you scold yourself. "If the cola can is somewhere around here, where would it be?"

"Probably in that jungle," you answer yourself.

You're not sure why you think that, but you do. Something tells you that all the island's secrets are hidden in and among those dense trees.

But so is the beast that keeps roaring.

What are you going to do?

If you decide to explore the jungle, turn to PAGE 7.

If you stay in the water, out of danger, turn to PAGE 32.

"You stole my ring!" Jenna growls.

"Yes!" you shout at her. "And I wish to go home! Now!"

Jenna throws her head back and lets out a terrible, moaning wail. You watch in awe as she begins to change.

Her whole face, body, and clothes slowly shrink back to normal size. She doesn't have razor-sharp fangs anymore. She transforms back to the way she was when you first met her.

Then her body starts to fade away — disappearing into a cloud of white gas.

"I suppose you're happy now," she whines. "Now that I have to squeeze back into that stupid can!"

You shut your eyes and brace yourself, not sure what's going to happen next. You recognize the familiar spinning feeling. Your wish is being granted.

But how will it turn out?

You never really got exactly what you wished for. What will happen this time?

Go on to PAGE 121.

"Follow me!" you shout to Peter.

Peter is too terrified to answer you, but he nods. You make a dash for it, knocking people out of your way as you go. You make it through the entrance to the food court and up an escalator before you look back.

You glance down and see that the crowd below you is beginning to scatter. They must have given up searching for you.

You and Peter keep your heads down as you weave in and out of the shoppers. You manage to make it to the parking lot without anyone recognizing you.

You've never been so happy to see a car in your whole life! You and Peter jump into the waiting Rolls Royce.

"Home!" you tell Manny. "Hurry — let's go home!"

"No way." Peter shakes his head. "Take me to my house. I'm not hanging out with you anymore. It's too dangerous!"

You plead with Peter to change his mind, but he won't. So Manny drops Peter off at his own house. Then the driver takes you back to the mansion.

You dread seeing James. You know you'll be in trouble for sneaking out. You wonder what James will do.

Find out how much trouble you're in on PAGE 35.

You give the driver Peter's address. Then you cast your eyes around the back seat. You spot a cellular phone. Plus a mini-bar, a TV, a laptop computer, and a CD player.

You grab the remote and notice a bulging wallet on top of the TV. Your eyes widen. It's filled with hundred-dollar-bills!

"Uh, excuse me." You lean forward to talk to the driver.

"My name is Manny," he tells you.

"Sorry," you say. "I don't know how I could have forgotten. So . . . um . . . Manny. Is the money in this wallet back here mine?"

"Of course," Manny replies.

All right! This will buy a lot of fries at the food court!

You tuck the wallet into your pocket, then pick up the cellular phone and punch in Peter's number.

"Peter!" you yell into the phone. "You won't believe where I'm calling from! Wait for me in front of your house!"

When the car pulls into Peter's driveway, Peter is standing by the curb. He watches as you climb out of the car.

You look up just in time to see his jaw drop open and his eyes bulge out as if they're going to pop.

"Peter, are you okay?" you ask.

But all Peter can do is scream! "AAAAAAAHHHHHHHHHHHH!"

Find out what's wrong with Peter on PAGE 109.

"Thanks," you tell the guy. You clutch the cola can tightly. You dart around to the back of the house and dash inside. The bug doesn't follow.

Yet.

"Jenna!" you call. "Jenna, where are you?"

"What's going on?" Randy rushes into the kitchen. Jenna is right behind him.

"Just wait," you tell your big brother. "You'll see."

"What's up?" Jenna asks. Then she spots the can in your hand. "You got it! That's the one! You got it!"

You let out a long sigh of relief. You have the right cola can.

"Okay, give it to me," Jenna orders you. "I've got to hold the can to get back inside. Then you can wish that you'd never met me — and everything will be all right."

"But what about the monster?" you cry. "That thing is headed this way! It will eat us all!"

"Don't worry," Jenna says. "Trust me."

Trust her?

Turn to PAGE 21.

You wait for Jenna to make her wish.

She fixes her eyes on you for a moment. Then she raises her arms above her head and throws her head back. "I wish that you were the genie, and I were free!" she bellows in a deep, booming voice.

"No!" you scream. But it's too late.

A jolt of electricity shoots through your hands, from the cola can, as Jenna says those terrifying words.

"NO!" you shriek again, collapsing in horror. But before you hit the ground, you feel yourself flying apart! It's as if your body is breaking into millions of tiny particles.

Jenna has vanished. And you have become a white gas cloud. Now you know how a tornado feels! You have no substance, but twist and swirl with great speed and power.

Finally, you spin faster and faster. The gas-cloud you've turned into gets narrower and narrower. You've twisted into a funnel shape, and started pouring down into the cola can.

You can't call for help — you can't speak! And you can't move — your body is all squished up. In the dark, cramped cola can, you can't see or hear anything.

Except the horrifying silence.

Turn to PAGE 132.

For sale? Did your parents move without you? Then it dawns on you. Maybe your whole family has moved with you to Beverly Hills. Now that you're famous.

Which means the cola can is gone!

Not sure what else to do, you climb back into your car.

"Take me back to the TV studio," you instruct the driver.

Maybe the cola can is there, you think. Maybe there's some way the can travels with you when the genie grants a wish.

Good theory. And guess what? You're right!

The cola can is sitting in your dressing room right this very moment. It's in a mini-bar in the corner of the room.

Too bad you're not there right now. . . .

Too bad there's so much traffic on the freeway. . . .

When you pull into the studio parking lot an hour later, you see Murphy, the guy who holds cue cards on your TV show. He's standing in the middle of a crowd — showing off his new Ferrari!

"That's strange," your driver says. "Murphy didn't have a Ferrari when he came to work this morning. He's not rich."

Then you notice a cola can in Murphy's hand . . .

Turn to PAGE 55.

But you can't stop your brother from blurting out his wish.

"I wish I could have the wildest, most amazing party ever," he says. "And I wish it were happening right now!"

WHOOSH!

You feel a sudden rush of dizziness, and for a moment the world seems to go black.

When you open your eyes, it's nighttime.

And your house is full of happy, noisy, partying high-school kids!

This isn't so bad, you think. Randy could have wished for something a lot worse.

You glance around the family room. You're standing in exactly the same spot you were before.

But the room has changed. It's lit by candles. Music blares from the stereo system, and mobs of kids are pressed against you, trying to shove and dance their way through the crowd. Everyone's drinking cola . . .

Hey! you suddenly think. Where's that cola can? The one Jenna came out of? The one she told you to be careful with. It was on the coffee table a minute ago.

Now it's gone!

Turn to PAGE 38.

You glance at Stephanie. She's frozen in place, staring at the Mortal Revenge fighters.

"AAAAAIIIIIEEEEE!!!!"

The thug in front lets out a piercing shriek and leaps forward. With a sharp, fast kick to your jaw, he knocks you to the ground. Then he spins and moves into a new striking pose, hovering above you. The other two creeps laugh.

You rub your jaw. It stings.

"I'll hold them off while you get away!" Stephanie cries. She bends over, grabs a garbage can lid, and hurls it at your attackers.

While they're looking away, you scramble to your feet and see an old, abandoned warehouse nearby — a good place to hide. You dash toward the door, yank it open, and duck inside.

And come face-to-face with the most terrifying sight of your life.

Your whole body shakes as you stare at the hideous creature. A four-armed ninja fighter — with the head of a rat!

Foamy saliva drips from the rat-man's mouth. He swings his arms wildly, holding a samurai sword in each of his four hands.

If you run back out into the street, turn to PAGE 52.

If you stay and try to fight the beast, turn to PAGE 105.

Use up a wish just to get rid of this guy? you think. You only have two left!

Nah. No way.

"No," you tell the big ugly genie. "I wish that — "

You hesitate, thinking about how to phrase it. What you really want, more than anything in the world, is for your first wish to work out just fine. You want to be rich — but normal. You want to be able to go visit your friends. Without being followed. Or being afraid.

But before you can say another word, the genie snaps his fingers.

POOF!

In a cloud of blue smoke, a giant fanged rattlesnake appears in the room. It raises itself up into striking position and hovers over your head. Venom drips from its fangs, and nearly splashes you.

You freeze in absolute terror. Every muscle in your body locks. You don't dare move.

The snake leans forward, hissing right in your face!

Turn to PAGE 10.

You've come this far. You're not going to turn back now.

As you step into the clearing, your mouth falls open. You can't believe what you see.

There. Right smack in the middle of the jungle. Five modern vending machines! They're arranged in a semi-circle around a tree stump, their lighted fronts glowing in the jungle shade.

A juice machine. A coffee machine. A candy machine. A milk machine. And a cola machine.

A cola machine!

"Yes!" you cry. Your face breaks into a huge grin.

Until you notice what's sitting on top of the cola machine. Then your stomach tightens again. It more than tightens. You panic. You're face-to-face with the beast you heard roaring.

And it's a tiger! A huge, angry tiger. A real one, with striped fur, sharp teeth and claws. Crouching. Ready to strike.

"Ignore the tiger," the parrot tells you.

Your heart pounds wildly. Is the parrot actually *talking* to you? Does it know what it's saying?

Or is it just repeating words it's learned before?

Do you dare to take the advice of a parrot?

The tiger leans forward. Drool drips from its sharp teeth.

If you turn and run back to the beach, turn to PAGE 134.

If you ignore the tiger and go for the cola, turn to PAGE 67.

"So you don't know where you are," you begin. You try puzzling this out. "And you don't know how long you've been here. And you've come here from different points in time. Is that it?"

The teenage boy smiles. "That's about right!"

"And you've never gotten any older?"

A girl wearing a long dress that makes her look like a princess steps forward. "I think I've been twelve for a very long time," she tells you. "There's something magical about this island."

That's for sure! A land inhabited by kids who never grow up? Wait a minute. You think you've heard of a place like this before. In some baby book. What was it again? Peter Pun? Pitter Pan?

Just then you glance up to see a little boy float·ing down to the ground. He's wearing green tights and green shorts. He has a little green hat with a feather.

"AAAHHHHHHHHHHH!" you scream in pure terror. It's him!

That's when you know you have reached a truly terrifying fairy-tale

ENDING.

The cola can must still be on the table in your family room!

You quickly change out of that goofy costume. You sneak out a side door to a parking lot. A long white Jaguar convertible is parked just outside. The driver smiles at you and gives you a nod.

Hmmmm, you think. Is that my car?

Well, you *are* a star. Maybe it is. You stroll over to the car and fling open the back door. You hop in.

"Take me home," you tell the driver. You rattle off your address so he'll know where to go.

"Huh?" the driver says, looking puzzled. "But that's not where you live. You live in Beverly Hills. In a big mansion."

Beverly Hills? Where the rich and famous live?

Then you realize. That must be your *new* house. Now that the genie granted your wish and you're a big star.

"No, no, no," you tell him. "I want to go to my *old* house. And step on it!"

Turn to PAGE 116.

104

Not enough money? How can that be? You handed her a wallet filled with hundred-dollar-bills.

"Are you sure?" you demand. You scurry over to the counter.

She nods grimly and holds out the bill for all the shoes. You take it from her and stare at it. You've never seen so many zeros in your life! It looks like you just bought a million dollars in shoes!

"How much is missing?" you ask. "How much more do I owe you?"

"Nine hundred and fifty-three dollars. And sixty-one cents."

Peter rummages around in his pockets. "I've got the sixty-one cents," he offers.

"Not funny," Cindy snaps. "You still owe me almost a thousand dollars. How do you intend to pay for this?"

You have no idea. But you can't tell Cindy that.

You glance at Peter. He shrugs. He doesn't have a solution either.

"Well," Cindy huffs. "I'll just have to call security."

"No," you plead. "I'm good for it. I promise. I'm rich. Really really rich. You saw my wallet. There's more where that — "

"Right," Cindy interrupts. "You probably stole that wallet!" She picks up the phone and punches in some numbers. "Security. Come quick! I've got thieves in my store."

Oh, no! Hurry to PAGE 131.

You are sick with terror. But you know that your only hope of survival may be to defeat this hideous beast.

The only way out of Mortal Revenge is to win. And this rat-faced samurai looks like the guy to beat.

The rat-man advances toward you. He swings the swords in all four hands, twirling them in a figure-eight pattern. They slice through the air, making a swish-swooshing sound.

You shudder. Those swords will slice right through *you* just as easily.

You take your eyes off the rat-man for just an instant. You glance around the abandoned warehouse, searching for a weapon. You need something to fight him with.

But the warehouse is empty! All you see is a pile of crumbling bricks.

Hmmmmmmm.

The rat-man opens his mouth in a disgusting hiss. His razor-sharp teeth drip with foam. His eyes glow red.

You've got to do *something*. Blood is pounding in your ears. Still he comes toward you, the blades slicing the air.

Then he pounces!

Quick! Turn to PAGE 84.

Randy doesn't even have time to finish his sentence. In an instant, your face is covered with pink-and-yellow stripes.

"I wish you'd shut your mouth!" you snap at Randy.

"No problem," Jenna says with a giggle.

Uh-oh. You've blurted out another wish without thinking. You glance at your brother. His eyes are wild. Full of terror. He's trying desperately to open his mouth. He pries at his lips with his fingers, tugging. Pulling. Twisting. No matter what he does, he can't get his mouth open.

"How's he going to eat?" you ask Jenna, your voice rising.

"That's *your* problem," she says with a sly smile.

Okay — think! you tell yourself. You've only got one wish left. What should you wish for?

Finally you decide.

"I wish you'd give me the rest of Randy's wishes," you tell Jenna. You think this is pretty clever, so you start to smile.

But Jenna just laughs. "Granted," she says. "But he doesn't have any wishes left! I didn't like him better than you after all. Ha-ha!"

Uh-oh. You just used up your last wish.

Oh, well. Your face is pink and yellow. But it probably should be *red* after all the mistakes you've made!

THE END

The butler gives you a small smile.

"You, of course, are at home," he answers in a formal English accent. "And I, of course, am James. In service to your family ever since you won the eighty-million-dollar lottery with that ticket your mother bought you. Are we having trouble with our memory today, if I may ask?"

"Yes. Yes, James," you mumble, trying to take all this in.

I'm rich! you want to shout. You feel like doing cartwheels and dancing around the family room. But you don't. James would definitely think you were nuts if you did that!

"Uh, James," you ask instead. "Do we have a car and a driver? I want to go see my friends."

James's polite smile disappears. His whole face frowns.

"Oh, no, no, no, no," he says, shaking his head quickly. "You can't do that, I'm afraid. You can't leave the house. It's much too dangerous."

Find out what happens next on PAGE 111.

"Awesome wheels," a little boy comments as you and Peter hop out of your Rolls Royce.

"Want to go for a ride in it?" you offer. You turn to the driver. "Okay, Manny? We won't be ready to leave for awhile."

"If that's what you want," Manny responds uncertainly.

"Great!" the little boy cheers. "Come on, Ma! Let's go!" He tugs his mother's hand. She smiles at you as they get into the car.

"Me too!" A man yells. "Can I go too?"

"Sure!" You wave your arms. "You can all go!"

The crowd cheers and then scrambles into the Rolls.

"That was fun," you tell Peter as the car drives away. "Now let's check out the mall!"

Do you want to go to the food court first? Turn to PAGE 17.

Or do you want to hit the sporting goods store? Turn to PAGE 81.

"AAAAHHHHHHH!" your friend Peter yells. "That is the coolest car I've ever seen!"

"I know. Isn't it awesome?" you shout. "And it's all mine. I'm rich! Peter, I'm rich!"

A neighbor, watering the lawn, glances in your direction. Two kids on bikes stare at you as they ride by.

Manny pops his head out the car window. "I wouldn't go announcing that to the whole world if I were you," he warns.

But why shouldn't you tell everyone you're rich? It's the truth, isn't it?

"I'm rich!" you shout again.

"I know," Peter exclaims. "I saw on TV that you won the lottery. Your face was all over the evening news."

You reach into your pocket, grab the bulging wallet, and pull out a wad of bills. You hand one to Peter. "Remember that dollar I owe you? Here's a hundred!"

Peter looks shocked. He gazes at the bill in his hand.

"Hop in the car," you tell him. "We're hitting the mall!"

Turn to PAGE 57.

You can't just let your little sister scream, can you?

Of course not.

So you forget the cola can.

You race through the dark house, down the hall, following the sound of her cries.

"Help! Stop it! You're scaring me!" Kate screams over and over again.

Turn to PAGE 114.

"You can't go outside," James tells you. "I am under strict orders from your parents not to allow you out of the house."

Is this guy for real? You're the richest kid in the world. You should be able to do anything you want. No way are you going to stay stuck in the house, you decide.

"Oh come on, James. I want to hang out with my friends. I won't be gone long. And my parents never have to find out. It will be our little secret." You flash him your best smile.

He doesn't smile back.

"Out of the question," he tells you. "I have my orders. I intend to follow them. And you will too."

"Okay, fine!" Obviously, you aren't going to get anywhere with this guy. "I'll stay here." Then you wave him away with your hand. "Uh, thank you, James. That will be all."

James doesn't move.

You let out a sigh. "Don't worry," you assure him. "I'm not going anywhere."

"Very good," James answers. He gives you a quick bow, then turns and walks out of the room.

You listen to his footsteps echoing down the long hallway. As they fade away, you pop your head out the doorway.

The coast is clear.

Sneak out of the house on PAGE 48.

You stare straight ahead, unable to move. You can't even blink.

You try to figure out where you are. The wall across from you is covered with paintings. But there's no furniture in the room. Nothing but a low bench.

Weird, you think. It looks like a museum!

"Ah!" a woman standing in front of you gasps. "Look at the shadows on the hair. So beautiful!"

People stop to stare at you, all right. And their mouths hang open when they see you. Just as you asked for in your wish.

Then the awful truth dawns on you. Your wish has come true — but not at all the way you had hoped!

You are beautiful, all right. Jenna has turned you into a beautiful painting! A painting so beautiful it hangs in a museum!

But that's not what I meant! your mind screams.

But there's no way to wish yourself out of this mess. You can't exactly open a cola can and let out a genie if you're frozen inside a painting. Or say the special wish-making words.

"Look at that painting!" a man in front of you whispers to his friend. "Isn't it beautiful? And so lifelike."

Being beautiful may not be all it's cracked up to be. Guess you're really hung up on your looks.

THE END

"Nooooo!!!!!!" A wail fills the studio. You glance at the audience.

Ooooops.

As far as those four-year-olds are concerned, Wilfred is a *real* dragon. Their hero. And you just ripped his head off! Right in front of them!

The noise in the studio is deafening. You realize you aren't only hearing upset, crying, screaming kids. You're hearing screaming, angry parents.

"You terrified my Clara!" a father bellows.

"You killed Wilfred!" a child weeps.

"What kind of cruel nut are you!" demands a furious mom in the front row. She takes a step toward you.

They *all* take a step toward you.

Back up to PAGE 50.

114

Kate's screaming is coming from the hall that leads to the kitchen. When you get there, a bunch of teenagers are crowded around, laughing and slapping each other high fives.

"Excuse me. Move it. Let me through!" you shout, trying to be heard above the noise. Randy must have used another wish, you realize. Now there's a live rock band playing in your family room.

Finally the teenagers move aside enough for you to see Kate, cowering outside a closet door, crying.

The minute she sees you, she runs up and throws her arms around your legs.

"They're scaring me!" Kate shrieks, still sniffling.

"Who is?" you ask her.

"Randy and these other guys," she whimpers. "They keep hiding in the closets and then jumping out to scare me!"

You give Kate a pat on the head. "Okay," you tell her. "Take it easy. I'll put you back to bed."

"No!" Kate whines, stamping her foot. "I won't go! I won't go! They'll hide in the closet in my room! And when the lights are out, they'll scare me more! You know what I wish?"

Wish? Did she say the word "wish?"

Uh-oh.

Turn to PAGE 24.

You've got to get rid of that monster!

"I wish the metal insect would go away forever and never come back!" you shout.

Then you close your eyes. And hope that you've said the wish right.

Because sometimes Jenna makes your wishes turn out all wrong.

When you open your eyes, everything is quiet.

You glance at the closet. It's empty. The metallic insect thing is gone.

Katie comes up behind you. She's smiling.

"Thank you, thank you, thank you!" she cries, giving you a big hug. "You are the best! I wish I had a hundred more brothers and sisters just like you!"

Uh-oh.

Did she just say what you think she said? Did she just make another wish? Yup. And *your* wishes are all gone!

Suddenly the house is overflowing with kids.

And they all look exactly like you!

Oh, well.

At least now you'll have some help when Randy decides to pick on you. You outnumber him a hundred to one!

THE END

116

Eventually, the white convertible pulls up in front of your old house — the one you lived in until about an hour ago. You leap out of the car and race to the front door, hoping that the cola can will be right where you left it.

But the front door is locked.

"Hey! Mom? Dad? Let me in!" you cry, pounding on the door.

No answer.

"Let me in!" you scream, jerking the door handle as hard as you can.

You peer in the windows — and your heart almost stops.

The place is empty. Bare. All the furniture is gone.

You glance over at the garage and gasp.

No cars. No lawn mower. No bikes. No gardening tools.

Empty. Everything your family ever owned is gone! Just vanished.

Then you notice a sign in the front yard. You barely saw it when you pulled up. Now you whirl around and stare at it.

FOR SALE.

Turn to PAGE 97.

"Let me shake your hand, kid!" the officer exclaims. "My wife and son had fun in your fancy car."

"Aren't you going to arrest them?" Cindy demands.

"Not a chance!" he tells her. "This kid is a millionaire. And generous too. You'll get your money, I can guarantee you that. As a matter of fact, how would you like a police escort, kid? Anywhere you want to go."

"Wow! A police escort!" Peter exclaims. "Like in the movies."

The people you bought new shoes for follow you out to your car, cheering. Everyone who got to ride in your Rolls Royce joins in.

You have Manny drive really slowly and turn the music up really loud on the built-in CD player. It's like a parade.

You've got a lot of money. And a lot of friends too. You use your second wish to throw a big pizza party. And your final wish to make everyone else a millionaire. What a nice kid you are. Guess this is one of those mushy, happy, feel-good

ENDINGS.

"Grant *your* wish?" you gasp, surprised by Jenna's words. "You want *me* to grant *you* a wish? But how?"

"Don't worry about it," Jenna snarls. "I'll handle the details. All you have to do is pick up that cola can and hold on tight."

You glance down and see the cola can lying among some twigs and leaves. You must have dropped it when Jenna came out.

"Pick it up!" Jenna orders again.

"Okay, okay," you say. "But then can I go home?"

Jenna's yellow cat-eyes narrow as she gazes at you. Her lips curl into a nasty smile, exposing her fangs again.

"When my wish is granted, you'll *be* home," she tells you.

You aren't sure what she means and you definitely don't trust her. But you don't exactly have a choice, stuck here in the middle of a jungle on some deserted island.

Your hands shake as you pick up the cola can and clutch it tightly. "Got it." You gaze, trembling, at the horrible genie. "Ready."

You prepare yourself for the worst.

What is the evil genie going to wish? Find out on PAGE 96.

I can't do it, you think. I can't use up my last wish!

If you do, you'll never be able to get rid of Jenna and get your mom back. And you're sure that getting rid of the genie is the most important thing in the world.

"*I* wish it!" Kate screams behind you. She has crept back into the hall. "I wish the monster would get out of here — RIGHT NOW!"

WHOOOOSH.

The world seems to spin. Just for an instant.

Then everything is so quiet you can hear the hum of the stereo amplifier in the family room. No music is playing. There's just a steady hiss as electricity buzzes through the amp and speakers, into the room.

The monster is gone.

"Way to go, Katie," you cheer, ruffling her hair. "You got rid of it! Good girl."

"Yeah," Randy says weakly. "Good job, Katie." He rubs his arm where the monster had gripped him.

That's when you hear it. Outside. The sucking noise. The shrill high-pitched whining and clicking sounds.

The screams.

Turn to PAGE 11.

Finally, slowly, the smoke fades away.

When it's gone, you suck in a big breath of fresh air. Then you glance around.

Wow! You're sitting in a fancy Hollywood dressing room — in front of a makeup mirror!

Is this *my* dressing room? Am I famous? Your heart beats extra-fast as you jump up, run out of the dressing room, and look at the door.

YES! There's a gold star painted on it! And under the star is your name!

"Thank you, Jenna!" you cry. "Thank you, thank you, thank you!"

For a minute you wonder where Jenna is. But you are too excited to worry about it.

"I'm a star!" you practically shout as you dance back into the dressing room. "I'm famous!"

You throw open the closet doors in your dressing room. You can't wait to see what kind of fancy clothes a big TV star wears.

But what you discover makes your stomach flip-flop.

"No way," you murmur, shaking your head. "This can't be right. No way!"

Turn to PAGE 56.

"Yes!" you cry happily, when you see where you are.

You're back in your own home. In your family room!

You jump up from the couch and dance around.

"What's up with you?" your older brother Randy asks, as he walks in carrying a tray full of snacks.

"Oh, nothing," you answer, smiling to yourself.

How could you possibly explain it to him? This is something you'll just have to keep to yourself. You'll remember it all your life, though. This was some adventure.

"Hey," you call to him, noticing all the junk food he's eating. "How come Mom's letting you eat that junk?"

"Mom's not home, idiot," Randy answers. "Remember?"

Then he points toward the kitchen.

"There's a whole six-pack of cola in the fridge too," he says. "Help yourself."

"Cola?" you repeat, your eyes growing large. "Uh, I think I'll pass on that."

Then something occurs to you. "But maybe I'll stash it in my room," you add.

"How come?" your brother asks, surprised.

"You never know when you're going to need a can of cola," you explain. "Sometimes nothing else will do!"

THE END

The warty genie breathes in your face again.

Yuck. Your stomach clenches from the smell. It's so gross. And so are his teeth. They're not just green and slimy. They're covered with moss!

He's right, you think. You *do* wish you'd never met him.

You back away from the huge genie.

"Yeah, okay," you tell him. "I wish I'd never met you."

The genie throws back his head and roars with laughter.

"GOOD!" he shouts. He opens his arms wide, then brings his hands together fast. When his palms touch, the force of his clap shakes everything in the pantry. Cans tumble off the shelves, dropping near your feet. Boxes of cereal begin to fall on your shoulders, your head.

Then suddenly, you feel yourself being lifted off the ground.

Turn to PAGE 128.

"Done!" you exclaim. The can is open.

"Nooooooo!" Jenna wails behind you. You turn toward her.

And gasp in horror.

"Aahhh!" you scream, stumbling backward.

Before your eyes, Jenna is changing! Fading. She's transforming into a ghostly version of herself.

You can see right through her. Through her skin, her blood, her organs. But you can't see through her bones.

Inside her transparent body she has a solid skeleton!

"What's happening?" you ask her, trembling.

"The can," she moans. She stretches out her long bones and fingers, pointing at it. It is a terrifying sight. She looks like a Halloween skeleton surrounded by a misty cloud. "You opened the can — and killed me! You've ended my life!"

She lets out another unearthly moan. Then she reaches for you. You shrink back against the kitchen counter, trapped. Just as her gnarled finger-bone touches your face, her body fades away completely. Only her skeleton remains.

The bones clatter to the floor.

Turn to PAGE 44.

"Stay away from me, you creep!" you yell at the metal bug.

You dash toward a group of Randy's friends who are all standing in the street, gawking from a safe distance.

"Listen, everyone," you pant as you rush up to them. "Did anybody take a can of cola from the family room? I need it back really bad!"

They stare at you as if you are crazy.

A short girl shakes her head. "A giant metal bug rampages through your house, and you're worried about a beverage?" she demands.

"Besides," a guy in ripped jeans adds. "It was a party! Everyone grabbed sodas."

"I know, I know," you answer quickly. "But I need a *certain* can. A special one. It was on the coffee table."

They obviously think you're nuts. Behind you, the insect crawls closer.

"Please," you beg. "It's important!"

Finally a guy in an orange T-shirt reaches into his jacket pocket and pulls something out. "Is this it?" he asks with a shrug. "I was going to drink it later."

You grab the cola can from the guy. Is it the right one? You have no way to know.

Turn to PAGE 95.

You wait, terrified of the moving eyes. They seem so eerie — just floating toward you in the dark.

Then you hear giggling.

Huh? Giggling?

"Hi!" a voice calls to you.

A moment later, the six pairs of eyes step right up to you — into the light at the opening of the cave.

It's just a bunch of kids. All about your age!

"Who are you?" you ask. "And how did you get here?"

"The same as you," a boy with glasses replies. "Bogus wishes."

"Yeah," a dark-haired girl says. "Each of us found that genie and wound up making the wrong wish."

Your mind races. "How long have you been here?" you ask.

They glance at each other. The tall teenager shrugs. "None of us knows. We've all come here from different times and places."

That's when you notice their clothing. Some of the kids are dressed just like you. But others wear strange old-fashioned outfits. And one girl seems to be in a futuristic space suit!

Turn to PAGE 102.

A girl approaches you. "I heard you were giving away hundred-dollar-bills," she says.

"Uh, yeah. I guess. Kind of." You aren't sure how to answer.

"Well, can I have one?"

You are startled by her request. Then you shrug. Why not? You're the richest kid alive. "Sure," you say and hand her one.

She stares at the money in her hand. Then she turns to the crowd. "You were right, Angie!" she shrieks. "This kid is giving away money!"

The room erupts! People rush at you.

"Hey!" you shout. "One at a time!"

But they don't listen. The crowd is screaming, tearing at your pockets. You are terrified. These people are crazy! "Help!" you shriek. Peter pulls you under the table with him. Together you crawl along the floor. The crazed mob overturns tables and chairs, searching for you.

"Now what?" Peter croaks, terrified.

"Back there!" You point at a hot-dog booth in the corner of the food court. The little store is dark and empty. It must be closed, but it looks like a great place to hide.

Or you could make a break for it. Try to outrun the crowd.

If you try to run, turn to PAGE 93.

If you hide behind the hot-dog counter, turn to PAGE 64.

"Back here!" the clerk cries. She leads you and Peter behind a counter, to avoid being trampled.

She eyes you curiously. You notice her name tag reads CINDY. "Are you seriously going to buy shoes for all those people?" she demands.

"You got it!" you answer with a smile. "I can afford to be generous."

So many people crowd into the little store that you and Peter help Cindy wait on the customers. Finally, the last kid brings a pair of sneakers to the counter, and Cindy totals up the bill. There aren't any more shoes left on the shelves.

You hand Cindy your wallet. "This should cover it," you tell her.

As she counts the money, you and Peter head for the door. "Sorry, Peter," you say, "no movies today. But we can come back later and — "

Cindy interrupts you. She holds up the wad of cash. "This isn't enough," she informs you.

Uh-oh. Turn to PAGE 104.

Your body tumbles in the air, over and over, as if you are being tossed and turned in a giant clothes dryer.

Finally, you drop to the floor with a thud. You glance around. "Hey, what? Why — "

Why are you back in your old house? Where's the mansion?

Then you remember your wish.

You wished that you'd never met the warty genie. So he sent you back in time — to before you even met Jenna! Before you wished you were rich.

Back to your old life. The life of a regular kid — not a millionaire.

No fair! you think. I didn't wish for that!

But then an idea hits you. Does that mean the cola can is still here? Maybe you can start all over! Make three new wishes.

And this time you'll get them right!

You race into the kitchen and yank open the refrigerator door. No cola. The fridge is empty, except for milk.

"Mom?" you call out. "Do we have any cola?"

"No," she answers. "Your brother just took the last one!"

You hear a familiar *"FZZZZZZFFFFFTTTT."*

Hope you've been nice to your brother lately. Because your chance to make wishes has just come to an

END.

A wooden baseball bat is no weapon against a metal monster, you decide.

Katie has managed to climb out the broken window. Randy is throwing everything he can at the insect. Books, games, sneakers — anything!

But still the monster comes toward you.

Time to make a run for it!

You dash out the front door.

SNAP! SNAP-SNAP! You hear the metal claws opening and closing wildly behind you.

You know what you have to do.

You have to find that cola can. Fast!

The metallic insect sticks its head out the window. It's looking for you!

It crawls back out the window after you!

Hurry to PAGE 124.

"Wait, Jenna!" you cry, dashing after her.

But it's no use. She's much too fast for you. By the time she's taken ten steps, she's completely disappeared.

Tired and frustrated, you drop to your knees. "I want to go home!" you moan. "I just want to go home."

Suddenly a voice startles you.

"You can't catch her that way," squawks the parrot. "Get up and ride the tiger!"

Huh?

You look up from the jungle path where you're kneeling.

The tiger! You'd forgotten all about him. You whirl around and see him still sitting in the clearing, near the vending machines.

He's sitting perfectly still, like an obedient dog who's been ordered to stay.

"Ride the tiger! Ride the tiger!" the parrot squawks.

Hmmm . . .

Ride the tiger. Does that sound like a good idea?

If you ride the tiger, turn to PAGE 27.

If you think it's safer to chase Jenna on foot, turn to PAGE 6.

Are you going to be arrested? You've got to get out of there.

But a second later a police officer steps into the store and blocks the exit. You're trapped!

"Are these the troublemakers?" the officer asks Cindy.

"Yes." Cindy glares at you. "They owe me a lot of money. And they're trying to get away without paying."

"We don't like that." The officer comes toward you, sneering.

"That one claims to be rich." Cindy points at you.

The officer bends down and stares you right in the eye.

You can feel sweat break out across your forehead. "But I am rich," you protest faintly. You smile weakly at him.

"Hey! I recognize you!" The officer stands up again. "You're the kid who let those people ride in your Rolls Royce, aren't you? The one that's parked out front, in the no-parking zone."

"Y-yeah," you stammer. Way to go, Manny! you think. As if you're not in enough trouble already!

Face the music on PAGE 117.

You wait for what seems like days. Years, maybe.

You have no way to know how much time passes while you are trapped inside the can.

You wonder if you will wait forever.

Then suddenly you feel yourself moving.

And all at once ... *PFFT!*

Someone pops the top on the cola can. Light pours into the tiny opening!

WHOOSH!

Without even knowing how you're doing it, you feel yourself breaking into a million tiny pieces, forming yourself into a gas-cloud. Then you shoot out of the can!

You're free!

As soon as you're out of the can, you materialize into a solid form, and cast your eyes around.

You are still in the jungle on the island. A kid dressed like a tourist is staring at you, his mouth wide open in shock.

You stare right back at the kid and say the only thing you can say:

"Hi! I'm a genie and you've got three wishes," you tell the kid. "Boom. Boom. Boom. Whatever you want. Three things — you name it, and I'll grant the wish."

Maybe being a genie won't be so bad after all.

THE END

"Sorry, Tiger!" you yelp. "I didn't mean anything! Good boy. Don't bite me!"

As if it understands you, the tiger stops snarling. It continues darting through the jungle at lightning speed.

You hang on tight. Pretty soon he catches up to the genie!

"What do you think you're doing?" Jenna looks shocked to see you. "Get off that tiger — right now!"

I won't do another thing you tell me to do, you vow silently. Ever!

Your fingers clutch the tiger's fur as it suddenly springs into the air. He leaps at Jenna.

"No!" Jenna shrieks at the attacking tiger. "Get back. NO!"

The tiger snaps at her face. But with her huge, powerful hand, she smacks it to the ground.

"Ahhhhh!" you cry as the force of her swat throws you from the tiger's back.

Turn to PAGE 34.

134

Ignore the tiger? No way, you think.

How could you possibly ignore a huge, man-eating beast whose powerful jaws are just inches from your head?

You turn and run. Run for your life. Feet pounding, legs pumping. And hope that the hungry beast won't catch you.

Mistake. *Big* mistake!

Here's how fast an average kid your age can run: 4.8 miles per hour.

Here's how fast a tiger can run: 30 miles per hour.

Get it?

Also, the basic rule of the jungle is: *Never* run!

Running always makes a wild animal think about chasing you.

Which is exactly what happens.

You run.

The tiger chases you.

You become a tasty little tiger treat.

Which happens to be exactly what the tiger was wishing for!

At least something got its wish.

THE END

"Hey! Way cool!" you shout.

You gaze around your new surroundings. Can this be real? Or are you just dreaming? Your heart races with excitement. Is this where you live now? It's a palace!

Well, at least a mansion.

You're sitting on a fancy black leather couch in a family room the size of a gymnasium. An elegant oriental rug covers the floor. A huge-screen TV faces the couch, filling one wall. Along the other walls are three different media centers, with enough computers, video games, and electronic music equipment to fill a department store.

A butler in a black tuxedo enters the room, carrying a silver tray.

"Would you care for an after-school snack?" he asks politely. Then he bends stiffly from the waist to offer you a selection of pizzas, soft drinks, candy, and apple juice — all your favorites!

"Uh, where am I?" you ask the butler, just to make sure. "And who are you?"

Turn to PAGE 107.

BAM! A door slams at the back of the house, startling you. Someone's home.

Wait a minute, you think. You already heard your mom's footsteps down the hall.

So who just came in?

You pop out of your room and spot your big brother Randy bounding into the family room. He's sixteen years old and really clumsy. Your mom says he's at an awkward age. His hands and feet seem too big for the rest of him.

Jenna follows you to the family room and flops down on the couch.

"Hi, Mom," Randy mumbles as he glances at Jenna. "What's up?"

Wait a minute — what did he just call Jenna?

Turn to PAGE 79.

"Hi," you say to your driver. His name tag says MANNY.

You try to act casual. "Uh, Manny, can you drive me to see my friends?"

"Of course," the driver replies politely. "Where to first?"

Great! The driver doesn't know about your parents' orders! You hop in the back seat before anyone else notices you.

But who should you go see? It's a toss-up between your two best friends, Peter and Stephanie. Peter likes to hang around at the mall. Stephanie likes to play video games.

Taking Peter to the mall could be a lot of fun. Shopping is probably awesome when you're a millionaire!

Then again, maybe you should pick up Stephanie and come back to the mansion to play video games. You saw that media center back there. It was out of control.

Stephanie's really good at video games. And she would totally be impressed.

"Where would you like to go?" the driver asks again.

If you go to the mall with Peter, turn to PAGE 94.

If you go pick up Stephanie instead, turn to PAGE 61.

About R.L. Stine

R.L. STINE is the most popular author in America. He is the creator of the *Goosebumps*, *Give Yourself Goosebumps*, *Fear Street*, and *Ghosts of Fear Street* series, among other popular books. He has written more than one hundred scary novels for kids. Bob lives in New York City with his wife, Jane, teenage son, Matt, and dog, Nadine.

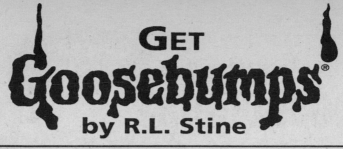

GET Goosebumps®
by R.L. Stine

❑ BAB45365-3	#1	Welcome to Dead House	$3.99	
❑ BAB45369-6	#5	The Curse of the Mummy's Tomb	$3.99	
❑ BAB49445-7	#10	The Ghost Next Door	$3.99	
❑ BAB49450-3	#15	You Can't Scare Me!	$3.99	
❑ BAB47742-0	#20	The Scarecrow Walks at Midnight	$3.99	
❑ BAB48355-2	#25	Attack of the Mutant	$3.99	
❑ BAB48348-X	#30	It Came from Beneath the Sink	$3.99	
❑ BAB48349-8	#31	The Night of the Living Dummy II	$3.99	
❑ BAB48344-7	#32	The Barking Ghost	$3.99	
❑ BAB48345-5	#33	The Horror at Camp Jellyjam	$3.99	
❑ BAB48346-3	#34	Revenge of the Lawn Gnomes	$3.99	
❑ BAB48340-4	#35	A Shocker on Shock Street	$3.99	
❑ BAB56873-6	#36	The Haunted Mask II	$3.99	
❑ BAB56874-4	#37	The Headless Ghost	$3.99	
❑ BAB56875-2	#38	The Abominable Snowman of Pasadena	$3.99	
❑ BAB56876-0	#39	How I Got My Shrunken Head	$3.99	
❑ BAB56877-9	#40	Night of the Living Dummy III	$3.99	
❑ BAB56878-7	#41	Bad Hare Day	$3.99	
❑ BAB56879-5	#42	Egg Monsters from Mars	$3.99	
❑ BAB56880-9	#43	The Beast from the East	$3.99	
❑ BAB56881-7	#44	Say Cheese and Die–Again!	$3.99	
❑ BAB56882-5	#45	Ghost Camp	$3.99	
❑ BAB56883-3	#46	How to Kill a Monster	$3.99	
❑ BAB56884-1	#47	Legend of the Lost Legend	$3.99	
❑ BAB56885-X	#48	Attack of the Jack-O'-Lanterns	$3.99	
❑ BAB56886-8	#49	Vampire Breath	$3.99	
❑ BAB56887-6	#50	Calling All Creeps	$3.99	
❑ BAB56888-4	#51	Beware, the Snowman	$4.50	

Scare me, thrill me, mail me GOOSEBUMPS now!

Available wherever you buy books, or use this order form. Scholastic Inc., P.O. Box 7502,
2931 East McCarty Street, Jefferson City, MO 65102

Please send me the books I have checked above. I am enclosing $_____ (please add $2.00 to cover shipping and handling). Send check or money order — no cash or C.O.D.s please.

Name_____ Age _____

Address_____

City _____State/Zip_____

Please allow four to six weeks for delivery. Offer good in the U.S. only. Sorry,
mail orders are not available to residents of Canada. Prices subject to change.